The Black Joke

FARLEY MOWAT

The Black Joke

ILLUSTRATED BY VICTOR MAYS

McClelland and Stewart Limited

The Canadian Publishers
McClelland and Stewart Limited
25 Hollinger Road, Toronto

Printed and bound in Canada

For Sandy and David
who will someday sail
to Miquelon

Books by Farley Mowat

People of the Deer
The Regiment
The Dog Who Wouldn't Be
The Grey Seas Under
The Desperate People
The Serpent's Coil
Never Cry Wolf
Westviking
Canada North
This Rock Within the Sea
  (with John de Visser)
The Boat Who Wouldn't Float
Sibir
A Whale for the Killing
Wake of the Great Sealers (with David Blackwood)

FOR YOUNG READERS
Owls in the Family
Lost in the Barrens
The Black Joke
The Curse of the Viking Grave

EDITED BY FARLEY MOWAT
Coppermine Journey
The Top of the World trilogy
Ordeal by Ice
The Polar Passion
Tundra

Contents

$\approx\approx\approx\approx\approx$

1

$\approx\approx\approx\approx\approx$

The Spences and the Ship

ONE wind-whipped summer day in the year 1735, a black-hulled ship came storming in from seaward toward the mountain walls which guard the southern coast of Newfoundland. All the canvas she could carry was bent to her tall spars, and she was closing on the rock-ribbed coast at such a furious pace it seemed inevitable she must meet destruction in the surf that boiled and spouted at the foot of the sea-cliffs.

Just over the horizon astern of her a squadron of French men-of-war was straining to overhaul the fleeing ship. Aboard the Frenchmen a hundred cannon were primed and loaded, waiting for the moment when the massed fire of the squadron could rip the black ship into fragments.

The fleeing vessel, sardonically named *Black Joke* by her master, John Phillip, was one of the most notorious privateers in Atlantic waters, and for two years French merchant shipping bound for Canada had suffered her plundering. But on this summer day the vengeful French naval squadron had almost trapped her off the island of St. Pierre, and now she was running for her life.

In the waist of the privateer stood a young man named Jonathan Spence. Two months earlier he had been an ordinary seaman on an English ship which had crossed the Atlantic to fish on the cod-rich grounds of the eastern Newfoundland coast. Spence's ship had been lying anchored in Acquaforte Harbour one day when the dawn light revealed the presence of a newcomer, a slim black vessel, lying across the narrow harbor entrance and commanding the anchored fishermen with her long brass cannon.

There was consternation in the fishing fleet as the officers recognized the infamous *Black Joke*. The captains had no alternative but to obey Phillip's "request" that their crews be mustered on the decks. And they could do nothing but look on miserably as he addressed the crews, promising good wages and high adventure in his service.

Phillip's audience was attentive. In those days the crews of fishing ships were little better than slaves. And so, when Phillip's bully-boat rowed away from the fleet, it carried the pick of the young and able fishermen; and amongst them was young Spence.

Jonathan Spence enjoyed his service with Phillip even though it was a life of hard sailing and occasionally of hard fighting. But Jonathan had a great desire to be his own master. He had already fallen in love with Newfoundland, wild and formidable as it was with its great inland mountains, sea-racked shores, and dark spruce forests. And he had made up his mind to settle on the island, never to return to England where starvation and a serf's lot awaited him.

But a settler's life on the much-frequented eastern shores was a precarious business at best, for the owners and officers of the English fishing ships considered the settlers to be intruders into their fishing preserves and the conflict between the two groups was often bloody.

Things were different on the south coast of Newfoundland. Here the deep fiords and coves were so well protected by off-lying reefs and shoals that fishing vessels seldom ventured near them. Only a few men knew the secrets of that coast — and Captain John Phillip was one of them.

His knowledge served him well on the day *Black Joke* fled from the French squadron. He held *Black Joke* upon her course even though the green hands in his crew were sure he was taking them all to their deaths. The massive sea-cliffs seemed close enough to touch, when suddenly a cleft opened in the rock wall ahead. It was a mere slit in the face of the mountains, but the black ship drove unhesitatingly into it and in an instant had vanished from the face of the gray ocean.

The slit, no more than a hundred yards wide, twisted and turned between thousand-foot walls until it ended abruptly in an almost circular harbor, half a mile in diameter. The harbor looked rather like the crater of an extinct volcano, except that its floor was sunk under deep water and the steep surrounding slopes were clothed in forests. Tumbling down from the high rim were several bright rivers, and, almost in the center of the crater, were two small islets between which ships could moor in perfect safety from any wind that blew.

Even before *Black Joke* had dropped anchor, Jonathan Spence had decided that this secret place was where he would make his home.

Jonathan had worked well during his time with Phillip and so, after vainly trying to persuade the young man to stay with the ship, the pirate skipper granted his request that he be set ashore. Phillip also provided Jonathan with tools, arms, and ammunition, and with sufficient stores to support him through his first winter. Three days later *Black Joke* sailed, and Jonathan was left alone in the harbor which Phillip had named Ship Hole.

Black Joke returned in the following spring to find a well-built cabin on the shore of Ship Hole and a healthy but exceedingly lonely Jonathan Spence rowing anxiously out to greet the pirate ship.

Jonathan's loneliness did not last long. A few days earlier *Black Joke* had captured a vessel bound for Quebec with a cargo of unwilling young women from France who were destined to become wives to the garrison soldiers in the citadel. The young women had begged Phillip to set them ashore in some free land and he had promised to take them to New England. But while the vessel lay in Ship Hole Jonathan caught the eye of one black-eyed lass who was ready and willing to join this sturdy young man in building a life in the Newfoundland wilderness. Phillip married the pair of them before he sailed, and from that day onward Ship Hole was never without the sound of human voices.

Two centuries after Ship Hole received its first inhabitants, a man who was Jonathan's namesake stepped out into the spring sunshine from the doorway of a two-story frame house overlooking the harbor. This latter-day Jonathan Spence was a square-built man in his forties, ruddy-skinned, and with shaggy brown hair shadowing his deep-set blue eyes. He looked what he was — a man of the sea.

On this spring day he gazed out over a familiar scene. The sun came streaming down over the surrounding cliffs and glinted from the white-painted walls of a dozen almost identical wooden homes which straggled along the south slopes. Ship Hole stood revealed as a typical Newfoundland fishing village, with its handful of houses facing the waterfront; its small square church, and the more imposing and concentrated cluster of buildings and wharves belonging to the local merchant. There were no roads in Ship Hole or vehicles either. Narrow, twisting paths connected the various parts of the settlement; but the sea was the real highway, and the whole life of the inhabitants depended on the sea. It was to the sea that the Ship Hole men went for their livelihood, for they were all fishermen, and it was by the sea that the only communications with the outside world were maintained. Inland lay hundreds of miles of mountain plateau and caribou barrens across which only the local Micmac Indians could make their way.

It was to the sea that Jonathan Spence's thoughts turned as he looked out toward the twin islets, between which a cluster of five schooners lay closely moored. They were two-masted fishing vessels; "laid-up" now, as they had been all winter, with their sailing gear stowed away on shore, so that they looked sleepy and abandoned in the bright spring sun. But there was one amongst them which stood out from her sisters as a ballerina would stand out in a crowd of folk dancers. Her slim, black-painted hull had a grace and delicacy which was unique amongst the rough-built, hard-working fishing ships. Although she was too far away for Jonathan to be able to read the name painted in gold along each bow, he knew it as well as his own. She was the *Black Joke;* and she belonged to him.

A vessel called *Black Joke* had belonged to each succeeding generation of Spences since the days when the first Jonathan came to Ship Hole in Phillip's pirate ship, and into the present *Black Joke* had gone all the experience and knowledge gained from generations of seamen and shipwrights.

Work on her had begun six years earlier, when Jonathan and his brother Kent had gone far back into the country to search out the trees destined for her timbers. It had taken weeks to find the right trees, to fell them and limb them, and to roll the logs down to the nearest rivers. In the spring the two men had rafted the chosen logs and towed them out to the coast where a trading schooner had picked them up and brought them on to Ship Hole.

Since there was no sawmill to do the work, Jonathan and Kent had to shape the timbers by hand, using axes and adzes exactly as the first Jonathan Spence had done. Planks to sheathe the timbers, two inches thick, ten to fifteen feet long, and often a foot wide, had to be whip-sawed out of solid logs — also by hand.

All that summer the timbers and piles of planks were left to season, and the following autumn the ship began to build. She took shape on a piece of relatively level ground between the house and the beach. Day after day the two men worked with their shipwright's tools, using only a hand-carved model of the ship for guide and plans.

They worked in any and every kind of weather; in bright sun, in snowstorms, and in blinding rain. By spring the frame was up and planked, and one fine day the ship was ready for the launch. The whole population of Ship Hole was on hand to watch and help as the wedges were knocked out from under her and she slid down wooden ways greased with rotted cod livers, and met the water with a mighty splash.

Among those who watched the launch, none was prouder than two small boys who shouted with enthusiasm when the vessel built by their two fathers rode off into the harbor as light and lovely as a gull. Peter Spence, who was Jonathan's son, was so carried away that he ran heedlessly down the ways, slipped on the cod oil, and shot out into the water in the wake of the schooner as if he was also being launched. His companion and first cousin, Kye Spence, Kent's only son, thereupon distinguished himself by throwing the first object he could find at Peter to help him keep afloat. Unfortunately the first thing he found was a stone net-weight. The stone was no help to the floundering Peter, but Kye's action gave rise to such a burst of laughter from the onlookers that the lad rushed home in tears and hid in bed. Here he was shortly joined by a chastened Peter, half-drowned and half-frozen, and wrapped in so many woolen petticoats belonging to his mother that he looked more like a rag doll than like a boy.

The launching of *Black Joke* was something the two children would remember all their lives. It was a lucky launching, and luck was with the ship.

When she had been fitted out and rigged, she sailed from Ship Hole with Jonathan as master and Kent as mate, and with a crew of four other local fishermen. She made her first fishing voyage to the far-off coasts of Labrador, and she was gone three months. When she returned, it was with a full cargo of salt cod in her hold. She had made a "bumper voyage." She had also proved herself to be one of the best and ablest sailers in the entire Labrador fishing fleet which numbered several hundred schooners.

The following year the brothers sailed her far out in the Atlantic to fish on the Grand Banks. Here she showed her worth to some of the best fishing vessels in the world, the big Banks schooners out of Gloucester and Lunenburg. Small as she was — she was only 80 tons as compared to the 200-ton Yankee and Canadian Bankers — she was able to carry sail in weather which forced the bigger ships to heave-to, and if there was another ship on the Banks that year who could catch her when she had a favoring breeze, *Black Joke* never met her.

On her first two voyages she made a considerable local reputation as a fast and lucky ship, but on her third voyage she made a name for herself right across the Atlantic. During the autumn of her third year afloat she made a charter voyage from St. John's, the capital of Newfoundland, to Oporto in Portugal with a full cargo of dried cod. Sailed by her two owners and a four-man crew, she made the passage clean across the western ocean in twelve days — a time not many big steamships could easily surpass. It was a passage that old John Phillip himself would have envied, and it made *Black Joke*'s name famous wherever sailing men got together.

As Jonathan looked across the harbor at her on this fine spring day, he should have been happy, but in fact he was deeply troubled. The great depression of the '30's was in full swing, and hard times had come to Newfoundland. Though the seas were still full of codfish, markets and money seemed to have vanished. Fishermen could hardly give away their catch, let alone sell it. In every outport it was the same story — near starvation, and growing debts to the local merchants upon whom the fishermen were dependent for the miserable rations of flour, molasses, and tea which had now become their staple diet.

Few of the merchants were generous men, and fewer

still believed in charity. In Ship Hole four of the five schooners belonging to the place had already passed into the hands of the local merchant, Simon Barnes, as part payment of their ex-owner's debts. *Black Joke* still remained free because the Spences had always fought shy of the merchant. The Spences had always paid their own way, for they had seen how easy it was to fall into debt to the merchant for food, clothing, or for fishing gear — and how difficult it was to escape again. They had observed that many outport people eventually came to be working for the merchant rather than for themselves.

Consequently, the Spence family bought little from Barnes, and sold even less to him. They preferred the adventurous alternative of sailing to St. John's each autumn with their summer catch of cod and selling it there. When they sailed home again, they would bring with them most of the supplies they would need in the year ahead.

The independence of the Spences did not endear them to Simon Barnes. Not only was he unable to make a profit on them, but their example was a dangerous one, for it tended to spread to other fishing families.

Jonathan knew perfectly well how Barnes felt, and he was worried. Ever since his brother Kent had been lost at sea during the annual seal hunt two years earlier, Jonathan had been hard put to keep things going. *Black Joke* was still free of debt, but Jonathan knew that unless he could find work for her, work that would bring in cash money, he would eventually lose her. He had thought of making a voyage to Labrador or to the Banks fishery — but what was the use of that when he would be unable to sell his fish for even enough to pay the cost of grub for his crew? He had thought of risking *Black Joke* in a voyage to the ice after seals, but the loss of his brother in a vessel even larger than *Black Joke* made him realize that this would be too foolhardy a venture. For a time he had hoped to be able to charter the ship to one of the big St. John's fish merchants for a spring voyage to carry salt cod to the Caribbean. With her reputation for fast sailing, she ought to have had no trouble finding charters; but merchants stick together, and Barnes had persuaded the merchants in St. John's not to give *Black Joke* an opportunity.

Jonathan was still staring at his ship, and puzzling over her future — and his own — when the door behind him swung open and he was almost bowled over as the two boys of the household, Peter and Kye, came bursting through the doorway wrestling fiercely with one another. Quick as a cat, Jonathan recovered himself and with one swift lunge grabbed each boy by the back of his homespun jersey.

They were an oddly assorted pair. Peter was lean and lanky with a wild mop of sandy hair and piercing blue eyes. His face was crimson with wind and sun, except for a thick band of freckles across his nose and cheekbones. By nature he was an enthusiast, often reckless, and usually heedless of the troubles he was storing up for himself.

Kye was of a different build: heavy-set and chunky

with lank black hair and a face as brown and round as that of an Indian, which was not surprising, for his mother, who had died when he was born, had been a Micmac from the nearby Indian settlement of Conne River. Kye was of a different nature from his cousin, tending to be more stolid and cautious, though he had a droll wit and an easy and engaging smile.

"By the Harry," Jonathan said when the lads had stopped struggling. "Is it bear cubs I have in this house —or b'ys? Answer me, ye whelps, or I'll skin ye and find out!"

He gave them both an affectionate shake that almost loosened their heads from their shoulders. Still panting, Peter wriggled in his father's heavy grasp.

"Leave be, sorr, please," he begged. " 'Twas just that Kye said *Black Joke* would have the dry rot afore we ever got around to givin' her an overhaul, and I told him 'twas *he* had the dry rot — in his head!"

Jonathan chuckled and released them. They stood before him looking sheepish. Good sturdy lads for their years, he thought to himself. It's a sad thing that Kent can't see his own boy now.

"Well, ye meant nothin' by it, Kye," he said aloud. "And ye may not be so far off the mark. The truth of it is I can see nothin' for the ship to do; no work at all. Still . . . that's no reason to neglect her. And broodin' and thinkin' won't keep her fit. It's past time we turned-to and got her into shape. Come on then, ye pair of connors! Down to the stage with ye and we'll do some proper work."

2

A Merchant Makes a Plan

FOLLOWED by the boys, Jonathan picked his way down the path toward the shore. It wound steeply between immense gray boulders that had scaled off the surrounding cliffs in ages past.

Each family owned its own stretch of beach from which the business of the cod fishery was conducted. A rough shanty, called the "fish store" or simply the "store," stood near high-tide mark and contained fishing and sailing gear, supplies of salt for making salt cod and, in season, piles of dry salt fish ready for market. Laid out haphazardly to shoreward of the stores were the drying flakes: flimsy platforms of spruce poles covered with boughs. On these the split, salted cod were laid to dry and cure during the warm summer days. Poking out into the harbor from each store was a rough-built dock of small logs decked with spruce poles. This was the "stage," where the fish were landed and where the men and boys gutted and split them.

One of the Spence dories — a flat-bottomed, high-sided boat about sixteen feet long — was moored to the end of their stage and while Peter and his father collected brooms, scrapers, brushes, paint, and tar from the store, Kye climbed nimbly down into the dory and began bailing out the accumulated rainwater. After loading the gear into the boat the others joined Kye, and the two boys took up the double set of oars and began to row toward the islets. They rowed standing up, leaning hard against the oars so that the narrow little boat leapt forward and in a few minutes was bumping her bow against *Black Joke*'s side.

Apart from a weekly visit to pump out her bilges, the ship had been deserted since the preceding autumn. When Kye pushed back the slider over the companion hatch leading down into her forepeak, he was greeted by a gust of damp, foul air.

"Whew!" he said. "Seems like we must have left half the fish in her last fall."

"Open her up, b'ys, open her up!" said Jonathan. "Let her breathe and she'll soon be sweet again."

The boys jumped to obey, opening ports and hauling off hatch covers to let the spring air into the dark lower spaces. Meanwhile Jonathan walked aft and, standing with his hands on her big wheel, let his eyes wander over his ship. He was seeing her, not as she was now, dirty and unkempt, but as she would be when she put to sea again.

She was not a big vessel — about seventy feet long on the deck line, if you did not count the big bowsprit which jutted out for another dozen feet. Just behind the bowsprit was a homemade anchor windlass and just aft of this again was the curved hood of the companionway leading down into the dark little forepeak where the crew lived and slept. The forepeak was like a cave, lit only dimly by a single round deadlight set into the deck overhead. It contained six narrow bunks in two tiers of three, a triangular deal table between the bunks, and a rusty stove. Apart from the deadlight, the only other illumination was supplied by an ancient brass lamp which swung in gimbals so that it would always stay upright no matter how much the vessel rolled or pitched.

Aft of the forepeak was the main fishhold, a cavernous black space stretching from the foot of the foremast to abaft the foot of the mainmast, a distance of nearly thirty feet. Dark as pitch, it stank of bilge water, salt fish, and wet wood.

Astern of the fishhold was the engine room, a tiny hold just big enough to take the old-fashioned single-cylinder gasoline engine which was the ship's auxiliary power. This "bullgine," as it was called, was twenty-five years old — an antique — but *Black Joke* was lucky to have even this aged monstrosity, for most of the coast schooners could afford no engine of any kind.

In the stern of the ship was a tiny cubbyhole known as the "master's cabin"; but this was only a courtesy title for it was so small and damp that the captain never used it, preferring to bunk and eat with the crew in the forepeak.

The helmsman stood right out in the open; and in heavy weather, salt spray burst over him with every sea that came aboard. As Jonathan stood at the wheel now, he could almost feel the spray in his face and, looking up at the bare spars, he could imagine a full press of canvas bellying to the gale as he had so often seen it on *Black Joke*'s long sea passages.

The thought that he might have to part with this ship, which he loved next to his own family, struck him with intolerable pain. Shaking his head to put the thought out of mind, he left the wheel and went forward to where the boys had already lit the galley stove in the forepeak and had placed a pot of pitch to soften on its top.

Once started, the boys and the man worked with a will. Equipped with a sharp, three-sided scraper, Peter was soon swarming over the vessel's upperworks, scraping away the peeling paint and laying bare the clean spruce beneath; and Kye worked in the engine room, oiling the old motor and repairing the bilge pump. Meantime Jonathan, equipped with a caulking mallet and a wad of tar-smelling oakum, was busy caulking the deck seams. As he finished each seam, he sent Peter below to fetch the pot of hot pitch, and then he carefully poured a fine stream of it into the seams, over the oakum. A little wind came curling around in the quiet harbor and the smell of oakum, pitch, and wood tingled in the nostrils.

All three were so engrossed in the pleasurable task of getting the ship ready for sea that they did not even look up when the *bumpu-bump-bump* of a single-cylinder engine came echoing across the still waters. A big open motor skiff had cast off from the elaborate wharf in front of Simon Barnes's store and warehouses, and was bearing down on the cluster of moored schooners. Standing up at the tiller was Simon Barnes himself, a lump of a man who had once been as powerfully built as an ox, but who had gone soft with many years of easy living. His jowls were whitened with a week-old beard, but above his craggy nose his black eyes still shone as bright and hard as those of a gull.

The motorboat came alongside *Black Joke* and Barnes pulled the switch to cut the motor just as Jonathan looked up. Barnes waved a hand.

"Morning, Skipper. Fine day for boat work, ain't it now?"

At the sound of the voice, Peter popped his head out of the engine room where he had been helping Kye to clear the suction of the bilge pump. His cheerful face hardened into a look of dislike as he recognized the merchant.

"Kye!" he called softly. "That ole dogfish Barnes's come alongside. Stand by to repel boarders!"

Pirate phrases and pirate thinking came naturally to both boys. They relished the ancient family association with Captain John Phillip, and the fact that the first *Black Joke* had been one of the most famous pirate vessels in Atlantic waters. Kye's reaction to Peter's challenge was immediate.

"All right," he whispered back. "You sneak out on

deck and slip the pump hose through the scupper where
he's got his boat. Give a kick on the deck when she's
all set . . . I'll do the rest."

When Barnes hailed him Jonathan answered politely,
for it is in the nature of the outport people to be polite
— even to those they do not like.

"It's a good enough day, Mr. Barnes . . . for any
kind of honest work," he replied slowly.

There was just the slightest extra emphasis on the
word "honest," but if Barnes noticed it, he paid no attention. He seemed determined to be amiable.

"Yiss," he said. "A fine day, indeed. Though it do
seem a pity, the time it takes a man to overhaul his
vessel, and no work waitin'. What you plan to do with
her this summer, Skipper Spence?"

Jonathan answered with calculated vagueness.

"Well now. That do depend. Might be I'll take a
voyage to the Banks. Then might be, again, I won't."
He stooped and deliberately began to pour a stream of
hot pitch into a seam, as if he assumed the conversation
to be at an end.

Barnes was irritated by the rebuff, but he kept his
temper.

"These do be right hard times, Skipper," he said
affably. "However, your name's as good as any on the
coast. A man would never lose on you. Anything you
need for fittin' out, now, you let me know. Anything
at all. You come alongside t'store and let me know. I
likes to see a man who don't give up easy. Yiss, sorr,
I likes to give a hand to a man. . . ."

He was suddenly cut short. With a gruesome gurgle a big rubber hose that had eased its way through a scupper hole under *Black Joke*'s rail, directly over the motorboat, began to jet a black and stinking flow that pulsed with every ounce of pressure Kye could exert on the rotary bilge pump. The solid mass of bilge water caught Barnes just below the chin. Staggered more by surprise than by the strength of the jet, he lost his balance and fell on one knee so that the water hit him square on the side of the face. His white stubble-beard turned black with old bilge oil and, as he opened his mouth to yell his anger, the filthy water trickled into it and almost gagged him.

From the deck Jonathan's stentorian bellow echoed across the harbor.

"PETER. KYE. LAY OFF THAT PUMP!"

The jet of water slowed to a trickle and then stopped. Kye turned to his cousin with wide-open eyes.

"We got him, Peter! We got him square! Only I guess now *we'll* git it too!" he muttered.

"Worth it, a million times," Peter replied; but there was a quaver of uncertainty in his voice.

On deck, Jonathan was leaning solicitously over the rail.

"Now that's a turrible thing to happen, Mr. Barnes," he said. "The b'ys never know'd you was alongside. I'll whop them good for bein' so careless."

Barnes had no answer that he could trust himself to deliver. Scrambling to his feet he bent and spun the flywheel of the engine and, as the boat got under way, he deliberately turned his back upon *Black Joke* and spat, with feeling, into the harbor. It may only have been, of course, that he was trying to get the taste of bilge water out of his mouth. . . .

As Barnes's boat puttered down the harbor, Jonathan called the boys on deck. They came slowly, dragging their feet and refusing to look at him. When they were only a yard away he said in his sternest voice of command:

"Look up, ye pair of tom-cods! Look UP, I say!"

Reluctantly they raised their eyes; only to find Jonathan standing with his legs widespread, and a grin on his broad face that no amount of self-control could master. Even as they watched, the grin spread wider and the big man slapped himself on the stomach and broke into a rolling bellow of uncontrollable laughter.

"Oh, ye young devils!" he sputtered when he could talk again. "Ye should have seen his *face*. . . ." But here a new wave of laughter overwhelmed him. The boys, knowing Jonathan of old, realized that there would be no sore seat for either of them and they relaxed, joining their mirth to his.

As he cut his engine to come alongside his own wharf, Simon Barnes heard the echo of that laughter and his fists clenched. He knew very well that the incident would become a story to be told against him for three hundred miles along the coast. Nevertheless, as he threw the mooring line to one of his clerks and climbed ashore,

Barnes displayed no sign of the anger he felt, for he had good reason to believe the Spence family would soon have little enough to laugh about.

It had been no casual visit he had paid to the *Black Joke* that day. His visit had been prompted by the contents of a letter which had arrived the previous night from St. Pierre, one of the three small islands still owned by France (and the last of her once-mighty possessions in North America) which lie less than twenty miles off the south coast of Newfoundland.

St. Pierre, a treeless, rocky island usually shrouded in fog, was a free port, which is to say that foreign goods could be imported and exported without payment of customs duties. As a result, it had been the center of a smuggling business for two centuries.

The smuggling had always been a local affair until prohibition was enforced in the United States in the 1920's. Then St. Pierre became the headquarters for an immense contraband liquor trade. Hundreds of thousands of cases of whiskey, brandy, and other spirits were landed there by big ships from Europe, for transshipment to rum-running vessels bound for the New England coast.

The resultant prosperity brought a building boom to St. Pierre, and most of the lumber required to satisfy it was supplied from the forests of Bay Despair, a multi-armed fiord which runs deep into the south coast of Newfoundland some thirty miles distant from Ship Hole. Control of this lumber trade fell into the hands of half a dozen south coast merchants, of whom Simon

Barnes was one. This trade brought him into close contact with several prominent businessmen on St. Pierre, and the letter which led him to pay his disastrous visit to *Black Joke* was from one of these businessmen.

This letter had come wrapped in an oilskin packet carried in the inner pocket of a St. Pierre fisherman's blouse. Two nights earlier this fisherman had landed his big sea-going motor dory on a deserted beach three miles from Ship Hole. There he had gone ashore and, with the aid of a carefully shaded flashlight, had located a pile of lobster traps stored in a cleft in the rocks. He had no difficulty picking out one particular pot which was marked with a splash of red paint across one end. Thrusting his hand into this pot, he found a thin copper box under the anchor stone, and in this box he placed the letter. Then he climbed aboard his dory which he and a companion rowed until they were well off shore. Only then did they start their engine. When dawn broke, it found them innocently anchored over a cod bank several miles off the coast, busily jigging for fish.

That same morning a man named Millar from Ship Hole was rowing his own small dory out of the harbor mouth. Millar too was a fisherman, though he never caught much fish — a fact which did not prevent him from getting unlimited credit at Barnes's store. As Millar came opposite the uninhabited cove, he was quick to see that the topmost lobster pot of the pile was now crossways to the rest. Casually he beached his dory and, after a good look about him to make sure he was unobserved, he ambled up to the pile of pots. An hour later he was sidling through the door of Simon Barnes's private office to lay a small package on the merchant's desk.

This unofficial postal service between Ship Hole and St. Pierre was not only quicker than the official one, it was also much more private, which, considering the kind of correspondence it carried, was no doubt just as well.

The letter described the current situation regarding the rum-running trade from St. Pierre to the United States. For a long time the rum-runners had used mother ships sailing from St. Pierre to points outside American territorial waters (which extend three miles seaward from the shore). Here the mother ships would rendezvous with fast motorboats which would then load up with contraband and slip it ashore at unguarded places on the New England coast. As long as the mother ships remained outside United States waters, the authorities could not touch them. As for the motorboats, they were so fast the revenue vessels could not catch them at all. It had been an excellent system in its time, but now — so the writer of the letter explained — things had changed.

The United States government had begun to wage all-out war on the rum-runners. A number of high-speed navy torpedo boats had been pressed into service. In addition, agents had been planted in St. Pierre, equipped with short-wave transmitters with which they could

notify the American authorities of the departure of suspicious vessels laden with liquor.

The result of these measures was to disrupt the trade.
Several of the fast motorboats had already been captured. The departure of a mother ship from St. Pierre
was now quickly known to the authorities, and these
ships were so closely shadowed that they had no chance
of approaching the United States coast in secrecy.

The situation was becoming desperate for the rum-
runners. Their warehouses at St. Pierre bulged with
tens of thousands of cases of contraband whiskey, repre-
senting a value of millions of dollars — if it could be
delivered in the United States. New smuggling methods
were needed, and so new methods had been invented.
The smugglers had now concluded that where speed and
power would no longer serve them, cunning would have
to be substituted.

Now for generations big fleets of sailing schooners
had put out each year from many New England and
Nova Scotian ports to fish for cod on the Grand Banks.
The sight of these comparatively slow sailing ships
beating heavily homeward with their holds full of fish
was a familiar one all along the Atlantic coast. These
fishing schooners had never been used for large-scale
smuggling attempts and no one ever suspected that they
might be so used. The rum-runners had therefore decided that certain chosen schooners, mostly small two-
masters, were now to be purchased and refitted for a
new "trade." False bottoms were to be rigged in their

fishholds, and they were to be given powerful diesel engines. By day, or in clear weather when there were patrol boats or aircraft about, these innocent-looking vessels would mosey along under sail alone. But at night, or when they had thick weather to conceal them, they would proceed under the full power of their new engines.

When they sailed from St. Pierre, they would apparently be laden with salt cod, or even fresh fish — but this cargo would only be a thin cover, and under it the main holds would be filled with whiskey. To all intents and purposes the schooners would look like legitimate fishing vessels bound either for New England ports with fresh-caught cod, or for Caribbean waters with salt cod. In point of fact they would proceed to secret coves and harbors on the American coast and there deliver their illegal liquor cargoes.

The rum-runners naturally wished to buy the fastest schooners available for their new venture, and it was inevitable that they would have heard about *Black Joke*. So it was that the St. Pierre representative of one of the American smuggling syndicates undertook to arrange for her purchase, and wrote his good friend Simon Barnes about it. His letter concluded with these words:

. . . and so, my dear Barnes, we can make an offer of very high price for this schooner. I myself think perhaps ten thousand dollars. If this makes an interest to you I am delighted to hear, but I will tell you we must have quick possession. The vessel should be delivered into St. Pierre before the first of June.

There was no question about Barnes's being interested in the proposal! Ten thousand dollars was an immense fortune in those times and in that place. The fact that he did not own *Black Joke,* and therefore could not sell her, was unimportant. He was now determined to own her.

Having read the letter for the third time, Barnes went to his office window, as if to assure himself that *Black Joke* was still moored behind the islets. Since there was no employment for her that he knew about, he had not expected to see the Spences at work fitting her out. The sight of the activity aboard her was unsettling. He decided he had to know what was afoot, and it was this which prompted him to visit her in his motorboat.

At that time he had some thought of attempting to buy *Black Joke* from Jonathan Spence, even though he knew in his heart that Jonathan almost certainly would not sell her. But after the encounter with the bilge pump he gave up any ideas he might have had of trying to acquire her by fair means.

Bathed, and changed into clean clothes, he sat at his desk once more, slowly writing a reply to his friend in St. Pierre.

3

The Dark Clouds Lighten

THE WEATHER remained fine throughout the following week, and work aboard *Black Joke* went forward rapidly. The upperworks soon glistened with fresh paint. The deck was tight again. The running rigging had been rove off and the vessel had begun to look eager and seagoing once more.

But now that the job was done, Jonathan again lapsed into a mood of dark depression. He was ready to work. The ship was ready. And there was no work for either of them. If nothing turned up in the next week or two, he knew he would be forced to go to Simon Barnes and ask for credit at the store; for his wife, Sylvia, had almost exhausted the supply of staple foods which Jonathan had brought in from St. John's the previous autumn. There was still lots of fish, both fresh and salt, but nobody can survive on fish alone, least of all the seven children who now lived in Jonathan's house. These included his own two girls and two boys, of whom Peter was the oldest, together with the three orphaned children of his brother Kent, led by Kye.

It was a quiet Saturday afternoon. Kye and Peter with some of the younger boys went up the harbor in a dory to try their luck fishing for sea trout. Sylvia, helped by her two young daughters, was finishing the dishwashing. Jonathan was sitting on the front steps, his eyes on *Black Joke* while he once again went carefully over all the possibilities for the employment of himself and his ship. He could think of nothing new. The only hope, and it was so faint as to be hardly worth considering, was that one or another of the St. John's fish dealers might have changed his mind about chartering *Black Joke* for a trip to Jamaica. Jonathan had laboriously written to these dealers again, begging them for work. An answer might be arriving on the weekly coast boat which was due that evening; and on this answer Jonathan pinned his final hopes.

Just before dusk the silent harbor came suddenly awake as a sonorous steam whistle sounded from beyond the entrance. The sound echoed and re-echoed from the surrounding cliffs. Doors burst open throughout the settlement as people began to pour out into the warm spring air. The children came first, racing wildly down the steep paths toward Barnes's wharf where the steamer would berth. Their elders followed more sedately, but by the time the little S. S. *Fortune* had poked her old-fashioned prow into the harbor proper, almost the entire population of Ship Hole was waiting for her on the dock. "Steamer time" was the great event of the week.

The mail was unloaded first and carried to the Simon Barnes store, for Simon was, amongst his many other roles, the postmaster.

Jonathan Spence was already waiting by the post office wicket.

"Letter for ye, Skipper," said Simon's clerk. "Come from St. John's, I do believe." He passed it across the counter.

Barnes, who had been standing nearby, quietly shifted his position so that he could watch as Jonathan moved away from the crowd, tore open the letter and studied its contents. Having had no formal education, Jonathan could not read easily, but he had no difficulty gathering the import of this reply to his pleading letter to the St. John's merchants. As he thrust the envelope into his pocket and turned toward the door, his face mirrored the bitter disappointment he felt.

"A moment, Skipper Spence," Barnes called after the departing Jonathan. "Can ye spare a moment, Skipper?"

Jonathan hesitated; he was in no mood to talk to anyone, but there was still politeness to consider. Reluctantly he turned about.

Barnes was too astute to refer directly to the letter, whose contents he had already guessed. Assuming his most amiable and friendly attitude he invited Jonathan into his private office.

When Jonathan emerged half an hour later he walked with the spring of a young man. His face was alight with eagerness and he almost ran up the long slope to his own home where Sylvia and the elder children were sitting by lamplight. The children were doing their lessons under Sylvia's direction, for there was no school in Ship Hole.

Throwing open the door and striding into the big kitchen, Jonathan caught Peter and Kye such a whack on their shoulders that they very nearly collapsed over their spellers.

"Enough o' that bookwork," he cried. "They's man's work to be done, me sons! Three days hence *Black Joke* goes to sea, and I'll be needin' willin' hands."

Pandemonium broke loose and it was some time before things quieted down enough for Jonathan to explain.

"'Tis this way, ye see," he began. "Ye know Barnes has collared the timber trade 'twixt Bay Despair and St. Peter's Isle. Well now, it seems he's got a rush order for timber for the Frenchies, and his own schooners won't be fit to sail for a couple of weeks or more. He's stuck, ye see. Stuck good. Anyhow, he's chartered *Black Joke* to make the trip. *And* somethin' more. The old dogfish agreed to give us three more charter trips if I'd help him out of a hole by taking on this one. He balked over that, but I told him straight I'd not shift a line until he gave his word, *and* wrote it out on paper too! And here it is."

He thrust a slip of paper under the lamplight and the family crowded around to spell out the words of the agreement written in the merchant's angular handwriting. Unable to contain himself, Peter grabbed the paper and began dancing around the big kitchen table.

"Ye're takin' Kye and me, Father," he cried. "Ye *said* ye were. I heard ye good!"

"Hush now," his father answered. "Ye'll have the whole settlement out to see what the row's about." He turned to his wife and, almost apologetically, continued:

"I know ye'll not like it, Sylvia. But ye see, I've no money for to hire a crew, and if I take a couple of men on shares, there'll be precious little left for ourselves at the end of the voyage. It's an aisy voyage. Inside-waters, the most of it, and a bare thirty mile of open crossin' to St. Peter's. I'll watch the weather sharp, and never sail unless it's fine. The b'ys are nigh onto bein' men, ye know. The three of us can work the ship. We *has* to do it — they's no other way."

Kye and Peter were closely watching Sylvia's face. The chance to make a voyage with Jonathan, not as deck boys or passengers, but as real crew, was almost too good to be believed. They hung anxiously over the table waiting for Sylvia's reply.

She smiled.

"There's no place to argue," she said gently. "The work must be done, and when there's not men enough, then b'ys must give a hand. Take a care, Jonathan; though I know ye will."

The Spence family was a long time going to bed that night. In celebration of their luck Sylvia made a huge lunch for them all, with pots of tea, and brown, crisp blueberry tarts. There was no longer any need to skimp.

Simon Barnes was also enjoying a celebration, though a much quieter one. Until nearly midnight he sat in his office, a bottle of contraband rum at his elbow, contemplating with increasing pleasure the ease with which he had persuaded Jonathan Spence to stick his neck into a noose.

A few minutes before midnight there was a gentle knock on his door. Barnes turned down the flame of the oil lamp before he opened to the visitor. It was Millar. Barnes gave him a letter-packet.

"Out with you now," he said. "The Frenchy'll be in to pick this up at the lobster pots soon as the moon is down. If you miss him, I'll have yer eyes for it!"

Black Joke duly sailed the following Tuesday morning. Her departure was a gala event. Every boy and most of the men in the settlement were on the beach to watch her go. The boys stared enviously at Peter and Kye as they nipped about the decks in answer to Jonathan's orders.

There was no breeze in the harbor so they departed under power. Kye had been given charge of the engine and on his first try he managed to spin the huge flywheel by himself and get the bullgine started. As it belched blue smoke from its exhaust, Jonathan gave his orders in a ringing voice.

"Let go aft — run her up to half speed, Kye!"

Kye, who had been standing with his head out the engine-room companionway waiting for the order, ducked below and shoved the throttle forward. The old engine thumped and jumped on its bed. The propeller churned, and slowly *Black Joke* drew away from the wharf and pointed her shapely bow toward the harbor entrance. On the steps of the Spence house Sylvia lifted a big conch horn to her lips and blew a blast of farewell that was answered by Peter, pumping the handle of the ship's foghorn.

The departure would have been perfect; except for one thing. *Black Joke* was carrying a passenger, and one of whom her crew did not approve. On Monday night Simon Barnes had sent a message to Jonathan announcing that he intended to accompany them on the voyage to supervise the loading and delivery of the cargo. It was a most distasteful prospect, but there was nothing Jonathan could do about it since his ship was under charter to the merchant.

Unfortunately for Barnes, he was no sailor. Even before the ship had cleared the quiet waters of the harbor and had begun to lift to the eternal swell of the open Atlantic, he disappeared from view to stretch himself out on one of the bunks in the forepeak.

"Fat ole landlubber!" Peter muttered to Kye as the two boys ran forward at Jonathan's command to begin hauling up the headsails. "Hope we git a hurricane. Might make him sick enough to die."

"Be no loss, I guess," Kye replied.

"Sway her up, b'ys," Jonathan barked from the wheel.

Slipping the halyard coil from the pinrack at the base of the mast, the two lads began hoisting the jib. It rattled and banged in the grip of a fresh southwesterly breeze that was beginning to blow, but they soon had it swayed-up and made fast, and the sheet hauled in so that the sail began to draw. The jumbo followed, then Kye went aft to take the wheel while Jonathan, helped by Peter, hauled up the big mainsail and the smaller foresail.

It was tough work for so small a crew, but all three were used to hard work and, though they were slower than a proper crew would have been, they managed the job in shipshape fashion. A few minutes after clearing the harbor entrance the engine was stopped and *Black Joke* was soon lying easily over on the starboard tack with all sails filled and drawing. The quartering breeze sent her boiling along at a good eight knots with a white bone at her teeth while to the north the great red coastal cliffs began to slide past.

It was a four-hour passage to the mouth of Bay Despair, but on such a bright spring day as this the boys could have wished it was forty hours. They stood alternate half-hour tricks at the wheel, for it was imperative that they should practice their helmsmanship. Steering a big schooner under all sail is not the easiest thing in the world. It is always necessary to keep a weather eye on the wind and the sails, watching for a shift, while at the same time trying to keep the vessel on a steady course.

Peter had been at the wheel about ten minutes when Jonathan came aft. He stood silent a moment, looking back at the ship's wake.

" 'Tis a funny thing, Peter," he said after a time. "There be no snakes at all in Newfoundland unless it happen there's one steerin' this here ship."

Surprised, Peter cast a quick glance astern. To his
horror he saw that the ship's wake, instead of being an
arrow-straight line, was more like a continuous letter S.
He began spinning the big wheel to straighten out the
wake, but the more he spun it, the more the ship swung

alternately from one side to the other of her proper course.

"Steady, lad," said Jonathan, amused at his efforts. "Be aisy with her. Just keep her sails full and by, and cock your eye on them islands up ahead to give ye a course."

Relaxing, Peter did as he was told and after a few more minutes the feel of the ship began to seep into him. He began to find himself so exhilarated by her motion, and by the knowledge that the whole eighty tons of her was as responsive as a child to his command, that he was soon steering instinctively; and the wake had straightened up behind him.

Meanwhile Kye had gone down to the forepeak to stir up some grub for dinner. He found Barnes still stretched out on a bunk. Tentatively Kye (who was secretly afraid of the merchant, as were all the boys of Ship Hole) cleared his throat and politely asked:

"Would ye feel like a bowl of fish and brewis, sorr? Missis Spence, she sent a pot of it on board for we 'uns."

Fish and brewis, which is a pudding-like mixture of softened ship's biscuits, salt cod and pork fat, is not the best thing to offer a man whose stomach is heaving with seasickness. But Kye did not know that, and he was shocked and enraged when the merchant answered with a particularly lurid curse.

Kye held back the angry comment he wanted to make, and, turning to the old stove, he soon had a roaring wood fire going. Then, deliberately and with malice aforethought, he took a frying pan and, half-filling it with thick slices of fat pork, set it to sizzling merrily on the stove. As if this were not enough, he soon contrived to spill some of the grease onto the stove lid where it sent up a billowing oily smoke which filled the whole forepeak.

There was a stifled groan from Barnes. Suddenly the merchant rolled off the bunk, staggered to his feet and made a rush up the companion ladder for the deck. Kye watched him go, with a wicked grin on his face.

"Maybe that'll teach ye to be more polite, ye old goat," he muttered to himself. Whistling happily he stowed the pan of pork fat in a locker and began warming up the pot of brewis and boiling the tea kettle.

By two o'clock that afternoon *Black Joke* had come abeam the mouth of Bay Despair. Now Jonathan took the wheel and brought the ship around on the other tack so that her course lay northward between Whale Rock and the mainland. This was not the main entrance but a shortcut or "inside" passage, full of sunkers (as reefs and shoal rocks are called in Newfoundland). It was the kind of place ships would normally stay well away from unless their pilots knew the waters well. However, Jonathan knew the passage perfectly, and he was anxious to get well into the Bay before nightfall so he had chosen the inside route in order to save time.

The passage through the sunkers was wildly exhilarating to the two boys. The ocean surge, bursting on the myriad reefs, sent great towers of spray billowing up on either side of *Black Joke,* and so close to her that wind-driven foam fell all across her decks. Boiling along with all sheets started, she was sailing so fast that an inexperienced observer would have been certain she was going to smash headlong into one of the unseen sunkers whose presence was revealed only by the swirling waters over them.

Barnes was not inexperienced, but on previous voyages, usually in his own schooners, his captains had carefully chosen the less spectacular passages. Despite his heaving stomach he was still able to take notice, and he was horrified at what he saw.

"Damn you, Spence!" he cried from his position hanging half over the lee rail. "Are you trying to drown us and sink the vessel? Get her out of this, you hear!"

Now, once at sea, the master of a ship is simply that — the master. Only a very foolhardy passenger, even if he has chartered the vessel, would dare criticize the master's judgment. The arrogance of this merchant in attempting to give him sailing orders was enough to fire Jonathan's temper to white heat. He managed to control himself, and he made no reply; but as far as he was concerned the brief truce between himself and the merchant — which had resulted from the charter — was at an end.

Clearing the inside passage, *Black Joke* ran down the main opening of the Bay past the little outport of Pushthrough and into the Lampidose Passage, whose towering cliff walls lead to the head of the bay and to the twin villages of Milltown and St. Albans. The wind held steady and an hour before dusk *Black Joke* was abeam of Milltown.

When the lines were fast to the wharf, and the ship settled for the night, Jonathan joined the two boys in the forepeak. Barnes had gone ashore.

It was Peter's turn to act as cook and he was just dishing up supper when his father climbed down the ladder and took his place at the table.

Jonathan looked at the two boys for a moment.

"For a pair of tom-cods with no brains and not much brawn, ye do all right," he said, smiling. "Give me a month or two, and I'll make sailors out of ye . . . or else."

Kye and Peter caught each other's glance. Neither would have admitted it, but they were as pleased as only two boys can be who have been told they can do a man's job and do it well.

~~~~~~~~~

4

~~~~~~~~~

Encounter with a Salmon

TUCKED snugly in their bunks, with the water lapping against the vessel's planks to quiet them after the day's excitement, the boys slept right through the early morning sounds of the lumbering town as it awakened. They did not hear the steam whistle at the ramshackle lumber mill screech its summons to the dozen or so men who operated the old-fashioned plant. They did not hear the high whine of the saw as it bit into its first log of the day. They were too dead to the world to hear anything — but they could still smell.

The sharp odor of boiling coffee seeped into Peter's sleeping thoughts. His nostrils wrinkled like those of a dog smelling a bone, then his eyes popped open and he was wide awake in an instant. Raising one foot he put it against the woven rope spring of the bunk above him and pushed hard.

"Hey, Kye! Quit poundin' your ear!" he shouted. "You goin' to sleep all day?"

Standing beside the stove, Jonathan watched the by-play with a smile. While the two boys tumbled out of their bunks and began to pull on their clothes, he dished up three huge bowls of cornmeal porridge and slapped them down on the cabin table.

"Eat hearty, b'ys," he told them. "We've ten thousand feet of lumber to stow afore dark. I wants to sail fust thing tomorrow mornin' while we still got fine weather. 'Twon't last forever."

The prospect of spending the whole day wrestling planks into the ship's hold thrilled neither boy. But it was man's work, and they were men — for this voyage at least.

"Yiss, sorr," they said in unison, and began shoveling the porridge into them.

Helped by a couple of men from the mill and watched with impatience by Barnes, the crew of the *Black Joke* soon got down to work. The rough, unplaned lumber came aboard in a steady flow while down in the hold Peter and Kye stacked it so that all the available space was used to best advantage. Their hands were soon filled with splinters, and the sweat ran down their backs, but they stuck to their task so well that an hour before suppertime Jonathan took pity on them.

"That'll do, lads," he said. "You can take the dory now and see can you catch a salmon for supper over to the mouth of Southwest Brook."

The boys needed no second invitation. Their aching muscles and sore hands were instantly forgotten. In a minute they had untied the dory, heaved their fishing gear aboard, and were rowing for the brook — a mile away — with as much vigor as if they had just jumped out of bed.

The salmon run had not yet actually begun, but a few early fish were to be found near the mouth of the rivers. Reaching the mouth of Southwest Brook, the boys anchored the dory in a deep pool and, while Peter leaned over the side to see if he could spot the black, twisting shadows of salmon, Kye paid out the jigging line from its wooden reel. This was a heavy twine, to the end of which was fastened the jigger itself — a cluster of big hooks whose shanks were bound together with sheet lead.

Kye lowered the jigger till it was a few feet above the bottom and then, with a rhythmic movement of his arm, he began "jigging" the little lead fish up and down so that it was constantly in motion.

Peering into the clear water, Peter saw an eel come swimming slowly up toward the jigger, then turn and slip down into the depths again. Two or three sea trout swirled around the jigger watching it with curiosity, though it was far too big for them to take.

Suddenly the trout vanished. There was a swirl of darkness and then a glint of silver as a big fish swam beneath the jigger and half turned on its side.

"Salmon!" Peter whispered excitedly. "Jig aisy, Kye! He's lookin' at it now."

The fish was probably not hungry, for salmon seldom eat much during the spawning run. But this one

was at least curious about the jigger which bobbed
slowly up and down before him. He hovered on gently
moving fins, facing the jigger for some moments; then
he lost interest and turned his back on the cluster of
hooks as if in complete disdain. But as the salmon's tail
curved past the jigger, Kye gave the line a strong upward jerk, and two of the hooks drove deep into the
salmon's flesh.

"Pull he up! Pull, b'y, PULL!" yelled Peter, but Kye
had felt the strike and was already hauling in the heavy
line.

"Give us a hand!" he cried. "This here's no half-dead
cod! The way he's chargin' around he's like to cut the
fingers clean offen me!"

There was no question of playing the big fish. The
line was too heavy for the salmon to break, and the
hooks were too deeply embedded to let him shake
them free. It was a trial of strength between the boys in
their rocking dory and a twenty- or thirty-pound fighting fish in his own element.

As the fish surged away under the dory, he dragged
the gunwale almost down to the water; and as Kye
stumbled backward to balance the boat, the line slipped
from his sore hands and the wooden reel rattled wildly
in the bottom of the boat while the line paid out with
a rush. There was no time for half-measures. With a
whoop, Peter jumped full-length to fall on the reel before the last few turns of line spun off it. Kye scrambled
to help him and for a few minutes they both sprawled
where they were, hanging on for dear life to the reel.

" 'Tain't no salmon down there, 'tis a whale!" gasped Kye. "Here, try and take a turn of the line round a thole pin afore he hauls us clean out of the dory!"

The tension on the line eased as the big fish changed direction. Peter took advantage of it to throw a turn around the pin while Kye frantically hauled in the slack. The next time the fish lunged away, the turn of twine around the thole pin acted as a brake, and the boys were able to ease the line out slowly.

The fight continued for nearly thirty minutes, but by then the salmon was growing tired. Once, he allowed himself to be hauled almost to the edge of the dory before he mustered his reserves and went charging off again. The boys had a good look at him before he surged away.

"By Harry," Peter said in an awe-smitten voice. "He's nigh as big as we 'uns. We'll never git he into the dory! Haul up the anchor, Kye, and see can ye row us to the shore."

While Peter hung onto the line, Kye recovered the anchor and, straining his muscles to the full, began to row for land. The salmon felt the motion and fought against it, so that Kye made slow headway. The dory was still a dozen yards from shore when the salmon, growing frantic as he felt himself being dragged into shallow water, made a supreme effort to escape into the depths. The dory swung half around and this time both boys lost their balance as the gunwale rolled down.

"Jump for it," yelled Kye, and, still clinging grimly to the jigger reel, he plunged into the icy water. Peter followed with an ungainly leap. Gasping for breath and splashing like two stranded fish themselves, the boys were now engaged in a straight tug-of-war with the great fish. But their feet were on bottom and slowly they inched backward toward the shore until the salmon, completely exhausted at last, gave up the struggle. In a few more moments they had pulled his glistening silver body up on the rough beach.

The boys had their fish, but that was all.

"The dory!" cried Peter as he looked up from a rapt contemplation of the salmon. "She's went and gone!" Sure enough the dory was placidly drifting off into the open bay accompanied, some distance behind, by a bobbing pair of oars.

Since neither lad was a particularly good swimmer, there was nothing for it but to hoist the salmon up on their shoulders and ignominiously make their way along the shore toward the little town. By the time they reached its outskirts most of the population had seen the drifting dory, and two men had already put off to rescue it. As the boys came along the waterfront they were met with joking remarks about, "Fishermen who trades their boat for a leetle salmon," and, "Lardy, b'ys, are ye practicin' to walk home from off the Grand Banks?" or, "Well, me b'ys, they's some can stay in a dory, and they's some as can't. Maybe the knack'll come to ye one day!"

The remarks were all good-humored, and Kye and Peter could grin ruefully in reply — until they reached the mill wharf where Simon Barnes was standing talking to Jonathan.

"You've no business puttin' to sea without a proper crew," Barnes was saying. "A pair of feckless b'ys what can't even handle a dory, ain't no crew at all. You'd best take my offer, and sign on Paterson and Wilson. Remember, if you loses any of my cargo, or damage it, there'll be not a cent of charter pay. And I knows you got no insurance on the ship. You'd best think it over."

The victory over the big salmon suddenly seemed like ashes in the boys' mouths. Without a word, they sneaked past the men, clambered over *Black Joke*'s gunwale and slid into the forepeak like a pair of beaten pups.

"We've spoilt things for yer dad," Kye said. "There ain't no salmon worth makin' trouble for him with ole dogfish Barnes."

When Jonathan descended into the forepeak a few moments later his face was set and stern, and the boys dreaded the prospect of what he would have to say. But they need not have worried.

"That's the finest kind of salmon ye got, me sons," he said. "And don't ye pay no heed to what Mr. Barnes was sayin'. Losin' the dory was somethin' anyone could do when he was fast to a fish like that 'un. Fact of it is, he's been onto me all day to sign on a couple of extra hands. Even says he'll stand their wages. But I knows the chaps he has in mind. Dock rats, the pair of 'em. They'll not come aboard a ship of mine. You youngsters is twice the men they'll ever be. So cheer yerselves

up a bit, lads, and one of ye git busy and carve off some
salmon chunks for supper. I'm that famished I could eat
the whole beast, head and all."

Their spirits restored, the boys jumped to obey, and
an hour later they were all sitting around the table,
stuffed with fresh salmon and at peace with the world.
But something still niggled at Jonathan's thoughts.

"Merchant Barnes was considerable anxious to git
them fellers took on board," he mused aloud. "Seems
like there's a bit of a stink in the air, and I don't like
it none. We'll keep our eyes skinned, b'ys. He might be
up to some of his queer tricks."

The next day dawned overcast and cool with a light
southeast wind. By the time the last of the lumber had
been stowed on deck (the hold was full by then) and
lashed securely in place, Jonathan had begun to glance
at the gray sky with some concern. A sou'easter in the
spring of the year could blow up dirty, as he well knew.
He was anxious to get away as soon as possible, but
Barnes did not arrive on the dock until nearly ten
o'clock.

"Step lively, if you please, Mr. Barnes," was Jonathan's greeting. "There's weather brewing and we 'uns
should be underway afore it hits. Unless you're a mite
nervous to sail with only the two b'ys and me?"

It was said politely enough but there was a sting to
Jonathan's words that brought a flush to the merchant's
face.

"I'll sail with the devil if I has to," he retorted

sharply. "But when a man asks for trouble like you're doing, Jonathan Spence, he's like to get it."

There was an ominous quality to Barnes's reply that made Jonathan's eyes narrow, but he said nothing more. Soon the lines were cast off and, as the ship's head swung away from the dock, the boys ran forward to crowd on the headsails. They moved smartly and, as the main and foresail gaffs rose on the masts, some of the men lounging on the lumber dock nodded their heads approvingly. Jonathan, at the wheel, noted their approval and he was pleased. The boys were shaping well, he thought, and once more he was glad he had refused Barnes's offer of a crew.

The run through the narrow channel, or "tickle," out of Milltown Bay was fast and uneventful. Close-hauled, heading as near to the wind as she would point, *Black Joke* snored through the water, her heavy cargo holding her steady. The wind freshened slowly as they ran on past St. Albans, past the mouth of hidden Roti Bay, and through another tickle into the Big Reach of Bay Despair. The rounded hills of Long Island, with their spruce forests in every valley, slipped rapidly past. Snooks Harbour came up abeam and Peter and Kye could see half a dozen dories anchored off shore, their crews busily jigging for cod. The boys waved gaily and the dorymen paused in their work to watch *Black Joke* go storming past toward the open sea. She was a sight worth watching. As the wind freshened she lay down to it a little, and the bone in her teeth grew bigger and whiter. Her red-brown sails bellied as hard as wood, and her slim black hull rushed through the water with the effortless grace of a porpoise.

Even Simon Barnes was somewhat moved by her perfection, and he found himself half wishing he could keep her for his own use, once he had gained possession of her. But the thought of ten thousand dollars in American currency quickly drove the idea out of his head. As he stood amidships, his back against a pile of lumber, he reviewed the plans he had made for *Black Joke*'s reception in St. Pierre. Jonathan's refusal to take on the two extra hands was a complication, for Barnes had counted on these two men, both of whom had long been in his debt, to help carry out his plans. Still, they were not absolutely essential. As long as the St. Pierre people followed the instructions given in Barnes's letter, nothing serious could go amiss. Barnes allowed himself a wintry smile as he contemplated the come-uppance which was awaiting that stiff-necked fellow, Jonathan Spence.

As *Black Joke* cleared the end of Long Island and encountered the Atlantic again, she began to rise to a head sea. The sky was a somber gray and the wind was still freshening. The ship's course lay southeast around the tip of Hermitage Peninsula and then across the bay to the town of Fortune, where all vessels outward bound for St. Pierre were required to clear through customs. It was a forty-mile run, but even with a head wind Jonathan could expect to make Fortune before nightfall. He remembered his promise to Sylvia, not to risk bad weather; but the ship was going along so well,

and he was so satisfied with the way the boys were settling down to their work that he decided to hold on
rather than put in to one of the nearby harbors for the
night.

As the ship came up to Pass Island Tickle, he laid her
on the compass course for Fortune and then called Kye
to take the wheel.

"Hold her steady, b'y," he said. "There's a fair good
breeze of wind blowin' and it may puff up. If a hard
squall hits ye, head her up into it until the puff is
gone. I'll slip below now for a bite to eat."

Alone on deck — for Barnes had again sought his
bunk, and Peter was busy getting supper — Kye stood
with his legs braced well apart, both hands holding
hard to the outer spokes of the wheel, and his head
cocked upward to watch the leach of the mainsail for
signs of flutter which would tell him he was pushing the
ship too close to the wind. He felt twice as big as he
really was, and twice as strong. Alone, in control of a big
ship in half a gale of wind (which was an exaggeration,
but one for which he could be forgiven), he would not
have traded places with the captain of the *Queen Mary*.

It was coming on dusk and the compass binnacle
lamp would soon need lighting, he thought. He glanced
down to check the course, found that the ship was
slightly off to nor'ard and gently eased her back again.
When he looked up, he was surprised to see a small,
rakish-looking steamer appearing from behind Pass
Island and heading on an intersection course with
Black Joke. Smoke was pouring from her stack as she

came on. It was a moment or two before Kye recognized
her, then he picked up a tin horn which hung from the
binnacle and gave a blast on it to call the skipper.

"Revenoo cutter, sorr," he yelled as Jonathan's head
appeared out of the companionway. "Comin' up fast on
the port quarter."

Jonathan joined him at the wheel, closely followed
by Peter. The three of them stared at the approaching
steamer with no friendly eyes. The government revenue
cutter was not popular with the south coast men, who
looked upon her anti-smuggling activities as an unjust
intrusion into their lives.

The steamer, rolling heavily in the seaway, was steering a course which would carry her across *Black Joke*'s
bows and no great distance off. As she drew closer, the
boys could see the figures of two or three men on her
bridge, one of them watching *Black Joke* through binoc-
ulars. On the foredeck stood a canvas-shrouded machine
gun, the sight of which made Jonathan spit over the lee
rail in disgust.

"The gov'munt says it can only pay starvin' folk six
cents a day to keep life in 'em," he said. "But they finds
money enough to send that tin-pot warship to stand
betwixt us and the cheap grub in St. Peter's. . . . Hold
your course there, Kye, hold straight on!"

This last was a direct order to Kye, who had begun to
ease the wheel over since it seemed to him that the
revenue steamer was going to cut dangerously close under *Black Joke*'s bows.

Peter, too, had seen the danger.

"She's comin' awful close in, Father," he said a little nervously.

"Yiss," Jonathan replied. "Close as she dares. Thinks she can bluff me into altering course to let her by. Well, me son, I ain't aisy bluffed. A sailin' ship has the right of way over a powered vessel. That's the law of the sea, lads, and don't forgit it. Hold her steady, Kye. He'll alter."

Kye's hands on the wheel were growing white with strain as the two ships continued to converge, each traveling at full speed. Even Jonathan had tensed, where he stood by the port rail. But he did not open his mouth to order Kye to haul away, even when the steamer, now less than three hundred yards off, sounded a demanding and penetrating blast from her siren.

A collision seemed inevitable, but at the last instant the revenue cutter heeled hard over as she made an emergency turn to port. *Black Joke* rushed on, and for a minute both ships were running almost side by side, and so close together that the boys could clearly see the face of the uniformed skipper of the cutter as he ran to the outer wing of his bridge, and, waving his fist at Jonathan, shouted down to him.

"Can't you keep that lumber scow out of my way, you idiot? We might have rammed you, and we should have, too!"

"Just you try it," Jonathan yelled back, "and the law'll have your master's ticket offen you quick as a wink — that is if you *got* a master's ticket, which I doubt!"

The cutter's captain could apparently think of no adequate rejoinder to this insult. The steamer dropped back until she could resume her course by crossing under *Black Joke*'s stern. By this time Kye's hands were wet with sweat and he was trembling.

Jonathan took the wheel from him.

"There's a lesson in this for ye, me sons," he said gently. "When ye're in the right of a thing, hang on. Don't change yer mind. There'll be many a time some feller what's bigger'n you, or maybe richer, or maybe just louder in the mouth'll try and shove you off your course. Don't take no heed."

It was good advice, and the day was approaching when Jonathan would wish that he had continued to follow it himself.

5

The Waiting Trap Is Sprung

THE WIND held steady throughout the remainder of the afternoon, and shortly before dusk the land loom of the Burin Peninsula began to show on the horizon ahead. Brunette Island came up fast and was left astern. The lighthouse on the end of the Fortune pier had not yet been lit as *Black Joke* came up into the wind a quarter of a mile off shore and hung there, her sails slatting until her crew had lowered them. The engine started with an explosive bark as Kye swung the flywheel and, with Jonathan steering, the schooner swung back on course and eased her way through the narrow entrance into the inner harbor.

Fortune's harbor seemed very small; but small or not, it was jammed with ships. At least twenty schooners lay moored side by side across the upper end, and another dozen lay alongside the wharves. These made up the Fortune banking fleet which would normally have spent the summer on the Grand Banks, dory fishing

NEWFOUNDLAND

MILLTOWN

SHIP
HOLE

BRUNETTE I.

MIQUELON

FORTUNE

BURIN PEN.

ST. PIERRE

for cod. But this spring the harbor had a deserted and abandoned look. There was no sign of life on any of the ships. No sails were bent to their spars. No running rigging stood taut and ready. Decks and upperworks were scruffy with neglect, and paint peeled from rails and planks. It was clear that hard times had come to Fortune as they had to all of Newfoundland.

"I mind the days," said Jonathan to Peter, who was standing by the rail, "when there was fifty vessels here at the one time. And all busy loadin' or unloadin' fish. A man could walk across the harbor on their decks. . . . Cut off yer bullgine, Kye. . . . Now, Peter, hop along for'ard and put a line ashore."

Black Joke kissed gently against the government wharf, and a few moments later she was securely moored for the night. Barnes hastened ashore at once. He had a telegram to send and one that brooked no delay. It was an innocent-looking message. Addressed to the well-known St. Pierre merchant, Jean Gauthier, it read:

EXPECT ME EARLY FRIDAY AFTERNOON WITH AGREED MERCHANDISE HOPE YOU PREPARED RECEIVE SAME PROPERLY — BARNES

Through the night, as the crew of *Black Joke* slept unaware, this message was being relayed by land-wire to St. John's, then to Placentia, where the trans-Atlantic underwater cable leaves Newfoundland for St. Pierre en route to Canada. Before dawn on Friday morning it had arrived in St. Pierre, and by breakfast time it was being read by Monsieur Jean Gauthier.

At about the same time that Gauthier was reading the telegram, Jonathan was reporting to the Fortune customs officer and getting his clearance papers for a "foreign-going voyage" to St. Pierre. It was only a formality, but a necessary one. Without proper papers it would have been illegal for him to land at St. Pierre. Jonathan believed in staying within the law, even if he did not always think the law was fair.

By 10:00 A.M. *Black Joke* was again under way. Overnight the wind had shifted easterly and though it had dropped light, there was still a good sea running. There was also the probability of fog, for an easterly wind often brings heavy fog in from the Grand Banks to blanket the eastern and southeastern coasts of Newfoundland. However, fog was no great threat to Jonathan. He had sailed in fog so often that he had developed a sort of sixth sense which seemed to enable him to find his way about.

They met the fog as they cleared the outer extremity of the Burin Peninsula at Danzic Point and took their departure from the land. It lay off to the southeast, a looming black wall that seemed as solid as stone. Rapidly it drifted down upon them, and before noon it had enveloped the vessel. Thick, wet, and icy-cold, it hung right down to the decks so that Peter, at the wheel, could not even see the sails above his head. Kye, posted as lookout forward, could not see fifteen feet ahead of the bowsprit as he strained his eyes through the curling murk. At intervals of three or four minutes, he pumped the handle of the bellows-driven foghorn. The deep blast of the machine seemed to be swallowed up at once in the dark and roiling mist.

Even Barnes came on deck. He made his way aft, and he seemed uneasy, pacing a few feet back and forward and staring up into the impenetrable fog overhead.

Thinking that the merchant was worrying about his cargo, and mastering his dislike for the man, Jonathan tried to soothe him.

"No call to mind a little fog, Mr. Barnes," he said conversationally. "We'uns'll raise the sound of the Green Island horn pretty soon. Still, it's your cargo and your charter. If ye say the word, we'll come about and run in under Danzic Head and wait to see will it clear off."

Barnes shook his head impatiently. "I'm not the man to worry about fog," he replied shortly. "But you might have to anchor in the Roads outside St. Pierre until it clears. I won't risk my cargo in the entrance channel in this kind of weather."

"There'll be no need to anchor, sorr. The breeze is haulin' northerly right now. By the time we stands in under the land she'll have blowed clear; or pretty nigh it anyway."

Barnes said no more, but his mind was busy. The fog might very well crimp his plans if it remained so thick that *Black Joke* could approach St. Pierre's harbor unobserved. On the other hand, a little fog would serve as a useful mask for what was planned. And much as he disliked Jonathan Spence, he had to admit that the man was a truly expert seaman. If he said the fog would be clearing by the time they reached St. Pierre, he was probably correct. Barnes decided to wait and see, but, with so much at stake, he found himself as restless as a cat. The blast of the hand foghorn from the unseen bow of the ship rasped his nerves. Turning on his heel he made his way to the forepeak, where he took a bottle of black rum out of his handbag, pulled out the cork, and raised the bottle to his lips.

Black Joke ghosted on through the fog. Between blasts on their own horn, Jonathan and the two boys strained their ears for the sound of another horn, either that of some unseen ship, or that of the powerful diaphone on Green Island. It was Peter who caught the distant murmur of the Green Island horn first. Cupping his right hand to his ear Jonathan listened for it too, and when it came again — *O-o-o-o-o-UMP* — he cast a quick glance at the compass and then smiled. "Three points off the port bow," he said. "Hold her as she goes, lad. We'll be abeam of the horn in half an hour and then we'll alter for St. Peter's."

Time slipped along. *Black Joke* altered to her final course, and Kye took the wheel while Peter relieved him as lookout. The light breeze had shifted to northeast and was making up a little. Soon the schooner would be approaching the entrance to St. Pierre's harbor and Peter, feeling the responsibility of his task, was already straining every nerve to penetrate the murk for a first sight of land.

He was not the only one who was staring out into the thinning fog that Friday afternoon. On the crest of the high hill which rises behind the town of St. Pierre and which commands a good view of the harbor approaches, a dark-faced man was waiting impatiently for the mist to clear enough so that he could use the telescope which lay across his knees. Near the foot of the hill, and within shouting distance of the man on the crest, a second man lay at his ease beside a motorcycle, smoking a cigarette and idly leafing through an old French magazine. From where he lay, a rough track led down to the town, joined the steeply descending streets, and ran on to the harbor side where a powerful but dirty-looking motor vessel, some sixty feet in length, lay with her dual engines gently ticking over. She was one of the fast American rum-runners, and in her wheelhouse Monsieur Gauthier sat nervously sipping a glass of brandy while opposite him the boat's captain, a big, broad-faced American named Smith, was absently toying with a heavy automatic pistol.

"There must be no possibility of mistaking things, *capitain*," said Gauthier in his stilted English. And, with a sideways glance at the pistol, "No monkey's stuff, you understand, with guns. The officials here are my good friends, but we must not make it difficult for them to be on our side. In New York, no doubt you would do things differently, but here you are in France. I implore you to remember that."

Smith gave him an amused look.

"You got nothin' to worry about, Johnny. Just do

your own job and I'll do mine. Soon as I get word from the boys up the hill that the schooner's comin', I'm off; and if I can't outsmart a hillbilly Newfie without usin' a rod, I'll quit the game. I'll make the whole thing look so good even that Newfie skipper'll end up thinkin' it was his own damn fault. The fog's clearin' off. You better git ashore — unless you wanta come along for the ride."

Hurriedly Gauthier set down his glass and scrambled to his feet. The last thing he wanted was to be aboard the rum-runner when she put to sea to carry out the plans of his friend, Simon Barnes. He was an organizer, not a doer.

As the Frenchman jumped agilely to the wharf, the American grinned disdainfully. "Frogs!" he muttered to his grease-stained engineer who had joined him on deck. "I'd give something to see that character turned loose on the New Jersey waterfront. The boys'd soon slice him up fer crab bait — him and his fancy talk!"

Black Joke was now close enough to the French islands so that her crew could hear the bleat of the foghorn on Galantry Head of St. Pierre. "Keep a sharp lookout, Peter," Jonathan commanded.

Peter did not need to be reminded of his duty. The fog was thinning and lifting, leaving scattered swirls of mist to obscure the surface of the water. As Peter stared ahead, he saw a darker loom.

"Land off the starboard bow!" he yelled.

"Good lad!" Jonathan shouted back. "That'll be Colombier Rock. Haul her off to south'ard, Kye, and keep yer eyes skinned for the channel buoy."

As the schooner closed with the land, the fog continued to fade until the outline of Grand Colombier Rock, six hundred feet high, stood clear and bold. Now the St. Pierre Roads — the open anchorage lying outside the harbor — began to appear. Farther away, and still somewhat obscured by mist, the high hills behind the town could be dimly seen.

"Time to shorten sail; there's a crooked channel ahead, and we won't want too much headway on the ship. Get the jumbo off her, Peter, then come and give me a hand with the foresail," Jonathan commanded.

As Peter brought the jumbo down with a run, Kye spotted the outer channel buoy and headed the ship toward it. Barnes, who had come on deck some time before, was standing in the bow looking fixedly toward the harbor itself.

"Nothin' to fear now, sorr," Peter said cheekily as he finished securing the jumbo and started aft to help his father. If Barnes heard the boy, he gave no sign; nor did he relax his attitude of expectation. Suddenly he leaned forward — yes, there was no doubt of it: coming slowly out between the twin piers of the inner harbor, a rakish-looking motor vessel was turning into the seaward channel. Barnes let out his breath as he recognized the rum-runner, then walked quickly aft.

"We'll have our lines ashore in half an hour," Jonathan said to Barnes as the merchant came up beside him.

"Maybe you will, Skipper, maybe you will," Barnes replied noncommittally; and leaving Jonathan to stare in surprise at his back, he moved to the foot of the mainmast and stood braced against it.

"Motor vessel comin' out the channel, Kye," Jonathan said. "Keep well over to the starboard side; give him what room he needs."

The two vessels were approaching each other fairly slowly, both on their own sides of the channel, which was now only a few hundred feet wide.

A sudden spurt of white water at the motorboat's stern caught Jonathan's eye. As he watched, the power boat leapt forward under the full thrust of her twin engines. In a few moments she was racing along at fifteen knots and then, quite inexplicably, she altered course directly for *Black Joke*.

With a single jump Jonathan was at *Black Joke*'s wheel, roughly pushing Kye aside. The motorboat was coming straight for the schooner's bow, and unless one of the two ships altered course a collision was inevitable. The action of the motorboat seemed so inexplicable that Jonathan wondered briefly if she had gone out of control — perhaps her steering had failed. He had only seconds to decide what he should do. If he hauled to port, and the other ship then tried to return to her own side of the channel, the consequent collision would be partly Jonathan's fault. But if he hauled to starboard and ran his ship outside the channel and into the nest of sunken rocks which lay there, he would probably sink her. The third alternative, to hold his course, trusting to the fact that *Black Joke,* being under sail, had the right of way over the other ship, might prove equally fatal unless the master of the motorboat quickly admitted *Black Joke*'s rights and swung back to his own side of the channel. It seemed fearfully plain that this was something he had no intention of doing.

There was no time to weigh the odds. The motorboat was holding straight on toward the schooner, and in seconds the two vessels would collide head-on and with disastrous results. Jonathan made his decision. With a shout of warning, he spun the wheel hard over and *Black Joke*'s bows began to swing to port, toward the center of the channel.

It was as if the master of the motorboat had been waiting for this action (as indeed he had). Having forced the schooner to disobey the rule of keeping to the right, the American now swung his own ship sharply toward mid-channel. Being under power, the motorboat answered to her helm much faster than *Black Joke* could do. Before Jonathan could counter this move by trying to swing back to starboard, the master of the motor ship had slowed his engines to quarter speed and had deliberately run under the *Black Joke*'s bow so that the schooner struck a glancing blow just abaft the rum-runner's wheelhouse. It was neatly done. The motorboat skipper had calculated the angle of impact to a nicety, so that his ship would take no serious damage. *Black Joke* swept along the rum-runner's port quarter aft. The schooner's anchor, catted out over her bow, caught on the rum-runner's boat davits and tore loose, plunging into the channel with a jolt that released the brake on the windlass and sent ten fathoms of chain running out with a roar. Brought up short by the anchor, *Black Joke* swung into the wind, her sails flapping wildly, while the motor vessel spun about and headed back at full speed toward the inner harbor, not even pausing to see what damage *Black Joke* had suffered.

Things had happened so rapidly that neither Peter nor Kye were at all clear as to what had actually occurred; but at Jonathan's shout of *"Get the sail off her. JUMP, you two!"* they leapt instinctively to the halyards. Meanwhile Jonathan raced forward and swung himself out on the bobstays (which brace the bowsprit), where he satisfied himself that, apart from two or three splintered planks well above waterline, *Black Joke* had taken no real damage.

The excitement seemed to be over almost as quickly as it had begun. While the boys furled the sails, Jonathan started the old engine. The chain and anchor were winched aboard, and the ship was under way once more.

Back at the wheel, Jonathan was reminded of the presence of the merchant, who had not moved from his position by the mainmast.

"You hit that poor chap pretty hard," Barnes said.

Jonathan could not conceal his surprise at the remark.

"Lardy, sorr!" he replied in astonishment. "He run

hisself square into *me!* A proper madman in command, I'd say. We's lucky not to be swimmin', with that'un out to sink us like he looked to be."

"P'raps *you* might see it that way," Barnes said, "but to me it looked like you went in the wrong, hauling over to port the way you did."

Jonathan's temper, already overstrained by the events of the past half-hour, shot out of control at this.

"Why, ye blind old robber!" he shouted. "In the wrong, was I? And what'd you have done? Hauled off to starboard and put the schooner on the rocks?"

Barnes only smiled coldly before turning his back and going forward to pack his gear.

Jonathan was still fuming when *Black Joke* entered the inner harbor and came alongside the wharf in front of the customs house. He was surprised to see what looked like a reception committee waiting on the dock. Apart from three uniformed *douanes* (customs officers), there was also a detachment of gendarmes led by the *chef de gendarmerie* himself. A score of civilians surrounded these dignitaries, but none of them offered to take *Black Joke*'s mooring lines when the boys flung them ashore. Kye had to leap to the wharf and make the lines fast himself.

Two of the customs men then came aboard, closely followed by the chief of the gendarmes. Jonathan led the way to the forepeak and, taking his ship's papers out of the watertight box where he stored his valuables, he presented them to the customs officers, while casting a curious glance at the gendarme. The police did not normally concern themselves with a vessel's arrival, and already Jonathan was beginning to smell trouble ahead.

The customs men made no difficulty. After a rapid reading of the papers, they excused themselves.

"All seems to be in order, but you will present yourself to the customs house, please, *monsieur le capitain*," said the senior of the two. "The formalities, you understand. Good morning." They climbed the ladder and disappeared, leaving Jonathan alone with the *chef de gendarmerie*, an imposing fellow in a most elaborate uniform. He seemed somewhat ill at ease.

"I am informed, Monsieur," he began, "that there was a little trouble in the channel?"

"Aye," replied Jonathan indignantly. "Trouble there was. I'll be takin' me protest to the harbormaster this very day. And there's like to be more trouble afore I'm through with that madman who nigh onto sunk my ship."

The policeman bowed very slightly.

"*Monsieur le capitain*," he continued, "I am afraid there will indeed be trouble. Already there is a protest lodged by the master of the other ship, and here is a writ from the *judiciairie*. Your vessel is under arrest until the matter is settled. You will not attempt to leave port, please? I am sorry. I must tell you, I do not like some of the Yankee people who come here in these times, but they have many friends in St. Pierre. I am not their friend, but I must do my duty. Let us go on deck, please?" He climbed the companion ladder with a worried Jonathan close behind him. One of the gendarmes had come aboard and was busy nailing an official-looking piece of paper to the mainmast.

"This man will stay aboard your ship," the Chief explained. "I hope he will not make the inconvenience for you."

Not a little confused by the course of events, Jonathan searched the crowd for Barnes, who, as charterer of the ship, would presumably be involved in any difficulties that had arisen. But Barnes had vanished. He was at that moment sitting in Jean Gauthier's living room, drinking a glass of neat whiskey and chuckling as he recounted the story of the collision.

"Went off smooth as oiled silk," he was saying. "That Yankee fellow — Smith you say his name is? — couldn't have done no better. So now there's him, and his crew, and me from *Black Joke* to testify Spence done the wrong thing. We'll all of us swear he had his engine going, even though his sails was still up. I figured on having two of my own men aboard to back up the story, but I don't reckon we'll need them. Spence won't have nobody but they two b'ys to testify for him, and both of 'em's too young to fetch any weight in court. How much did you tell Smith to ask fer damages?"

"Fifty thousand francs," Gauthier replied amiably. "It will be enough, for you tell me Captain Spence has no money. My *avocat* has arranged all. The official investigation will be held on Monday, and there is little doubt of the result. After that will come Smith's suit for damages. If we win that, then the boat will be sold to pay the judgment, and already it is arranged that I will buy the boat. A week, no more, is needed. I have been able, as you say, to oil the wheels of justice a little."

6

The Land Sharks Snare a Ship

JONATHAN SPENCE was more angry than unhappy. He was not much worried about the outcome of the investigation into the accident. That would get straightened out easily enough, thought Jonathan. But he was annoyed that the master of the rum-runner had had the nerve to pretend total innocence and attempt to lay the blame on the *Black Joke*.

"We're in a kettle of fish, b'ys," he explained to Peter and Kye, whose curiosity about the presence of the policeman was so great they could hardly contain themselves. "See that bit of paper the Johnnydarm has nailed onto the mainmast? That's what they calls a 'blanket.' It's a kind of summons, like. Means *Black Joke* is under arrest, but they can't very aisy put a schooner into their jail, so they sticks up that poster on her and puts a guard aboard to see she don't run off."

"But why'd the Frenchies want to arrest *Black Joke?*" asked Peter.

"On account of the so-called skipper of that cock-eyed motorboat what almost sunk us. Knowed he was in the wrong, so he hustles into harbor ahead of us and swears out a complaint claimin' 'twas we 'uns was at fault. Tryin' to git the leap on us, ye see. But we've no cause to worry none. With ye two young 'uns and merchant Barnes to back me up, the truth'll come out quick enough. We'll have that seagoing idjut wishin' he'd stayed t'home to drive a pony cart, when the truth gits told. I'm off to the agent now to see about gittin' the cargo took off. Ye b'ys stay close to the ship till I gits back."

Jonathan leapt onto the quay and walked briskly across the *Place,* a large open square beside the harbor which was enclosed on three sides by the offices of ships' agents (who conduct the shore business for visiting ships), bars, cafés, and shops catering to fishermen and seamen. Several idlers glanced at the big Newfoundlander curiously. The story of the collision in the channel was already common gossip.

Jonathan turned into one of the larger buildings, under the gilt-encrusted sign of *Jean Gauthier et Cie,* and striding up to the ornate counter he caught the attention of a rather seedy-looking little man behind it.

"Captain Spence," he said firmly, "Schooner *Black Joke* come from Bay Despair with lumber belongin' to Simon Barnes. You speak English?"

The seedy little man smiled briefly. *"Oui, monsieur* — yes, *mon capitain,* I speak it very well. We already have the order from Monsieur Barnes to act as agent for your ship. Tomorrow the stevedores will unload the lumber. Meanwhile whatever we can do to be of service, you must ask. There are supplies perhaps you need?"

Jonathan shook his head. "Maybe afore we sails for home there'll be some things to buy. Main thing you can do fer me now is find out exactly why my vessel's been arrested. That, and tell me the course I ought to steer with the authorities."

"Certainly, Monsieur. As to the first, I can myself tell you what you wish to know. *Monsieur le capitain* Smith, whose ship you hit, has made the protest to the harbor authorities that you cut across his bow incorrectly and without warning. Besides he has made the action against you in the court for damages — very large damages I think, perhaps fifty thousand francs.

"Two days from now will be the investigation at the *Palais de Justice*. It will be best for you to have an *avocat* — how you say, a lawyer? There is, of course, the matter of the cost. It will be necessary to deposit five thousand francs, to guarantee the fee of the lawyer."

"Five thousand francs!" Jonathan replied indignantly. "That's close by a hundred dollars! Almost more'n me charter's worth! Where d'ye think I'd lay hands on that much money, eh?"

"As to that, Monsieur, I cannot say," said the agent smoothly. "Nevertheless, no lawyer will act for you without the guarantee. Perhaps Monsieur Barnes will make the advance against your charter?"

"And perhaps codfish'll start to fly! Look 'ee here, me

son. I'm in the rights in that collision, and it don't take a hundred dollars to help me tell the truth, neither!" And with that Jonathan turned on his heel and stamped out of the building, while the agent lost no time in picking up the old-fashioned phone in his office to inform his employer, Mr. Gauthier, of the details of the encounter.

Gauthier and Barnes were still together. After having listened to his employee on the telephone, Gauthier turned gleefully toward his guest.

"It marches well," he said. "The good *capitain* will not find anyone in St. Pierre to help him with his case — unless he pays; and pay he cannot unless you wish to be the generous friend and make an advance upon his charter."

Barnes chuckled and poured himself another drink. "That sounds likely, don't it now?" he asked.

Aboard *Black Joke,* Peter and Kye were doing ship's chores, furling the sails in proper harbor style and generally putting things shipshape; but they could not refrain from casting longing glances at the town.

It was the largest town either of them had ever seen and, though it only boasted five thousand people, it seemed like a veritable New York. Trucks laden with salt fish trundled busily through the *Place.* Other trucks laden with wooden boxes, stenciled with the names of famous whiskey manufacturers in Scotland, were shuttling back and forth between the whiskey warehouses and a rusty old tramp freighter which was unloading at one of the docks. Basque fishermen, wearing black berets, brought their big power dories laden with fresh cod into the harbor. Motorcycles roared and sputtered up the steep and narrow streets past gray and weathered houses built in the styles of ancient France. A steady stream of apparently aimless loungers moved in and out of the several bars along the waterfront. One group, consisting of three or four tough-looking men carrying sheath knives at their belts, wandered down to the dock where *Black Joke* was lying, and eyed her speculatively. Ignoring the two boys, who were at work loosening the lashings on the piles of lumber stowed on deck, they began to talk amongst themselves.

"Them Newfies sure build 'em rough," one of them said.

"Rough but tough, I guess," replied a second.

"Good enough lines to her," said the third. "Give her the power and she'll move."

The first man laughed harshly. "Yep, she'll move. Move right out from under that tinhorn Newfie skipper. Who do you reckon'll take charge of her?"

"Smith, more'n likely. He's welcome. For my money she's a fish tub, nothin' more, even when they put a hundred horse-power diesel in her guts."

"Lay off that talk," said the first man. "This joint's getting lousy with Federal agents. Keep your yap shut, Jimmy, or someone'll shut it for you."

"Who's to hear? Nobody aboard her but a French cop with hair in his ears and a couple of kids. Hey, kids, you hear what we been sayin'?"

Peter and Kye had heard all right, though they had

not fully understood. They were a little afraid of these strange men who spoke English with a queer accent, so they pretended total ignorance. Ducking their heads they continued with their work.

"See?" said the man who had been told to keep his mouth shut. "Deaf and dumb. Dumb, anyhow."

Nevertheless the three men continued their conversation in lowered tones that no longer carried to the boys' ears. After a few minutes they re-crossed the *Place* and entered another bar.

When they were out of earshot, Peter turned to Kye.

"Can 'ee figure what they 'uns was talking about?" he asked.

Kye shrugged: "Sounded like they was plannin' to buy *Black Joke,* or thought they was anyhow. You think maybe they're rum-runners from the States?"

Peter nodded his head wisely. "Must be. Good thing Dad wasn't aboard or he'd have made 'em swallow what they said about Newfoundlanders."

Jonathan did not get back to the boat until late afternoon, and when he did arrive he was in no happy mood. After leaving the agent's office, he had gone to the offices of three different lawyers and had tried to arrange for one of them to represent him at the official hearing into the accident. The first lawyer had simply refused to understand English, though Jonathan was certain the man understood it well enough. The other two had been agreeable to represent Jonathan — if he was prepared to give them a retainer of a hundred dollars in advance.

"I never thought too much of lawyers," Jonathan told the boys when he got back to the ship, "but I never figured to find them squeezin' blood from a man *afore* they'd give him a hand. I'd have told the lot of 'em to go to perdition, only I run into a skipper I knowed, Paddy Mathews from Burin. His vessel's lyin' up on the marine railway for hull repairs and he got me aboard of her and told me he figures I either got to git a lawyer, or lose the case. He claims he heard a story someone's plannin' to steal *Black Joke* offen me, and has paid off the authorities to help. Paddy's a good man, and worth trustin'. So after he told me that, I went huntin' for merchant Barnes. Took me two hours to track him down. I asks him for half the charter money in advance, seein' as how the lumber is safe delivered in St. Peter's. Barnes says, 'Your charter ain't completed until we gits back home, Skipper Spence, and I never pays until a job's complete.' Well, b'ys, I wasn't goin' to beg offen the likes of him so I come away, and here I am."

Kye and Peter looked at each other, not quite sure whether to risk adding to Jonathan's problems or not, then Kye took the bull by the horns.

"There was somethin' happened whilst you was away, Uncle Jonathan. A crowd of Yankees or some such fellows come down to the wharf — rum-runners likely from the look of them — and Peter and I heard 'em talkin' like they expected friends of theirs was goin' to own *Black Joke*. One of 'em said somethin' about 'movin' her right out from under her Newfie skipper.' "

"Don't pay no heed to half what ye hear, me b'ys," Jonathan said, for he did not wish the boys to know how worried he was becoming, and how their story dovetailed with what he had already heard from his friend, Mathews. It was all rumor, of course, but the rumors were beginning to make a pattern — one that Jonathan did not like at all.

Affecting an air of joviality, Jonathan put the boys to work getting supper ready. After it had been eaten and the enamel plates and mugs had been washed and carefully stowed in the racks above the old stove, he announced that he was going ashore once more.

"Goin' to look for a old friend of mine," he explained. "Fisherman from Miquelon, name of Pierre Roulett, married a woman from the south coast. He used to come down the Bay years past, salmon fishin'. Me and Kye's father done him a good turn once when the fishery patrol boat was looking for Frenchy poachers. He always said if ever I come to St. Peter's I was to seek him out, and now I guess it's time I did. Seems like we could use a friend or two."

The boys waited up until late that night, but Jonathan did not return until after sleepiness had driven them to their bunks. In the morning he told them that he had been unable to find his friend, Pierre Roulett. "He's off in Miquelon where he belongs to," he explained. "Him and his son Jacques. So it looks like we'll just have to make out on our own."

Soon after breakfast a gang of French navvies appeared on the wharf with three old trucks, and all through the day they worked the lumber. By the afternoon the decks and holds had been cleared and *Black Joke* lay empty.

At dusk another gendarme came to relieve the one on duty guarding the boat, and he brought a paper for Jonathan — in French. When Jonathan took it to the agent for a translation it turned out to be a summons to appear at the *Palais de Justice* at 10:00 A.M. on Monday to attend an investigation of the collision.

Unable to find another soul in St. Pierre who seemed willing to lend him even moral support, Jonathan called on Paddy Mathews to accompany him and the two boys to the inquiry. The four of them sat ill-at-ease on a hard front bench in the dusty old judicial hall while the proceedings commenced. These were all in French, and no effort was made to translate them into English. When Jonathan got to his feet and protested that he might as well be back on his ship, for all he understood of what was going on, he was told sharply by the President of the Court — who spoke excellent English — that it was his own fault for failing to obtain the services of a bilingual lawyer to represent him.

But several of the witnesses spoke English. The first of these was Captain Benjamin Smith, the skipper of the rum-runner.

Grinning broadly, Smith stood before the table occupied by the President and two harbor officials, and when he was asked to tell his story, he did so with gusto.

". . . So there we was, headin' down-channel nice

and careful and legal-like, and mindin' our own business, and givin' that schooner plenty room, seein' as how
she *seemed* to be under sail. We was a couple hundred
yards from her when my mate notices smoke comin'
from her exhaust pipe, so we knew her skipper was
usin' his engine to help him along. About then, for no
reason I could figure, he shoves his helm hard over and
comes sheering right out into our side of the channel,
cuttin' straight across our bow. I swung off to starboard
as hard as I could but it was too late and he plows
square into us and damn near cuts my ship in half. I
turned and beat it for the harbor quick as I could,
figurin' we'd sink any minute. We only just got her
back to the wharf and put a couple auxiliary pumps
aboard in time to keep her afloat. The way I see it, the
schooner skipper must have figured we didn't know he
had his engine running, and was just plain ornery
enough to try and make us give way to a vessel under
sail. . . ."

Jonathan's rage, when he heard this piece of bare-
faced lying, was too much to control. He leapt to his
feet and in one stride had reached the American. His
hand shot out like a striking snake and caught the
Yankee by the right shoulder. Shaking him as easily as
he would have shaken a rabbit, Jonathan roared at
him:

"That's . . . a . . . ruddy . . . lie . . . and . . .
ye . . . knows it!"

Caught off balance, and wincing from the pain of
Jonathan's grip, Smith seemed paralyzed. Before he

could recover, three gendarmes had surrounded the struggling pair and separated them. Jonathan was forced back against a table and held there while the President delivered a stinging rebuke and threatened to eject him from the court if he misbehaved again.

The President and the two officers who sat with him barely seemed to listen to the rest of the evidence, simply nodding their head as if in agreement with everything Smith's crew members had to say.

But the worst was yet to come. After the last of the rum-runner's crew had testified, each following his captain's lead, Simon Barnes was called to the stand.

He did not look at Jonathan. He kept his gaze on a spot on the ceiling as he described exactly the same situation Smith had already described. When he had finished, the President asked him whether or not the engine of *Black Joke* had indeed been running at the time.

"Yiss, sorr," Barnes replied without hesitation. "Captain Spence, he started it up just after we passed the outer channel buoy. It was runnin' about half speed, and no mistake."

This time nothing but the firm grip of Paddy Mathews, plus the fact that Kye and Peter were clinging to his coatsleeves, kept Jonathan in his place — but nothing could make him keep quiet. His roar of anger must have been heard over most of St. Pierre and even the magistrate seemed a little intimidated by it. At any rate he did not carry out his threat, but called Jonathan to the stand instead.

"You may now give your version of the affair, *monsieur le capitain*," he said coldly, "and perhaps you will be able to control yourself."

"Indeed, sorr, I'll tell me story," Jonathan cried. "In the face of that whole lot of lyin' savages and a hundred more of their black-hearted kind —"

Here the President banged his gavel hard on the desk. "I've warned you already, *capitain*," he shouted at Jonathan. "This is the last time. Your story, please, and nothing more!"

Jonathan managed to get a grip on his emotions. Slowly and fully he described exactly what had occurred in the channel. The President asked no questions and made no comment. Soon after Jonathan had returned to his seat it became obvious that the hearing was over, and that the three-man panel was now deliberating over the verdict — though all in French.

Once more Jonathan interrupted.

"Are ye not going to hear the b'ys?" he asked. "Ye've listened to a pack of thieving wharf-rats. Will ye credit them ahead of these two lads?"

"They are mere children," the magistrate replied sternly, "and as such cannot give evidence in this inquiry. And you, Monsieur, have been warned often enough to behave yourself. Remove him!" This last was directed to the gendarmes.

In a matter of moments Jonathan found himself hustled outside into the street, accompanied by the boys and by Mathews.

"Well," said Mathews, wiping his brow and spitting

angrily on the steps of the *Palais*. "If that's what they Frenchies call justice, I be powerful glad I lives somewhere else."

Jonathan had now mastered his rage and had become dangerously calm.

"There's no two ways about it," he said. "They've made up their minds to find me in the wrong. The whole shebang's been all one piece of trickery, aye, even the collision itself. And I was the blind bat what never saw the light till now. Some feller ought to wallop me over me thick head with a saw log. Come aboard with us, Paddy. There's only one thing left for a man to do, and I be thinkin' I may need a hand."

The two walked off at a fast pace toward the dock while Kye and Peter trotted along behind.

"What'll yer dad do, do ye think?" Kye whispered breathlessly.

"Dunno," said Peter. "But whatever it is, I hopes nobody gits foolish enough to stand in the way of him when he does it!"

When they were all in *Black Joke*'s forepeak (with the scuttle tightly closed to ensure that the gendarme, in case he understood English, could hear nothing), Jonathan began to talk.

"It's clear enough," he began. "Barnes give me that charter to git me over here, plannin' all along to make me lose the ship. He fixed that collision, and I don't doubt he's got it fixed to buy the ship back from the Frenchies for a song. Ever since he fust come to Ship Hole he took a black stand again we schooner men haulin' our salt fish to St. John's and buyin' our grub there 'stead of from him. What with the hard times, he's already got his hands on four of the Ship Hole vessels, and he must have made his mind up to git all five, and finish me into the bargain.

"Well, me sons, he ain't goin' to do it. I'm not fool enough to think I got a chance of fightin' him legal-like in St. Peter's. So that leaves just one thing to do. We're goin' home, without a by-yer-leave, and the devil take them all and their Frenchy justice.

"Paddy, you've been the finest kind of friend, and I don't want to draw you into this here mess wuss than you are right now. If I git away with what I'm plannin', the Frenchies ain't goin' to like any man what helped me. But I wish ye'd do one thing for me, if ye will. Can ye git a few of your lads out about midnight, play-actin' like they was blind drunk, and have 'em start a row in behind the Customs House? Most of they French Johnnydarms knocks off work at suppertime, and there won't be none of them about to quiet down the ruckus. With a little luck, the feller on guard aboard of us will figure he has to do somethin' about the fuss ye makes . . . and all we needs is a quarter-hour free of him, and we're away."

Mathews nodded his head.

"Me name ain't Paddy for nought," he said happily. "We'll start a row as'll draw a policeman right clean out of his uniform. Leave it to us, Skipper."

"Don't ye overdo it now, Paddy. We don't want to scare yon poor Johnnydarm to death, ye know. Just draw him offen the vessel for a bit. And meantime, mum's the word."

After Mathews had left, Jonathan and the boys began working out the details of their plan.

As soon as dusk began to fall, Kye and Peter were to wander along the docks to the shipyard where a number of rowing skiffs were moored. Casually they were to borrow one and row it about the harbor as if they were just out for a little fun. But as soon as it was full dark, they were to row very quietly to *Black Joke*'s bow and hide the skiff in the shadow of the vessel, mooring her to the schooner's forward bitts.

At midnight, when Paddy Mathews and his men had drawn off the gendarme, Jonathan and Kye were to jump into the skiff while Peter cast off *Black Joke*'s mooring lines. Then the two in the skiff would tow the schooner away from the wharf and into the tide race which would be running out of the harbor at that hour. Tide and skiff together could be expected to move *Black Joke* to the mouth of the inner harbor in short order. Once clear of the harbor piers, Jonathan and Kye would come back aboard and the engine would be started. It was probable that no one ashore would notice the sound of the engine but, if they did, they would think it was only a motor dory bound out early for the fishing grounds. In any event, by the time an alarm was given and a crew could be found to man a vessel in pursuit, *Black Joke* ought to be safe outside the three-mile territorial waters of St. Pierre.

"We've luck with us at the start," Jonathan explained.

"There'll be no moon tonight. We has the tide to help us, and from the look of the weather, no wind to hinder us when we tows her past the piers. Suppertime now. Eat good and hearty, b'ys, and tomorrow we'll be sailing into Fortune Bay."

7

A Flight at Night

JONATHAN's admonition to eat hearty was wasted on the boys. The prospect of stealing their own ship away from the French authorities left them with no appetite at all. When Jonathan went aft to check the engine in preparation for their attempt, Peter and Kye burst into a gabble of talk.

"We maybe ought to try and git that Johnnydarm drunk, Kye," Peter suggested. "Real pirates used to do that kind of thing."

"Might git him *too* drunk, then we'd never git he to go ashore at all," replied Kye cautiously.

Jonathan, just descending the companion ladder, caught the last part of the conversation.

"Aisy, b'ys," he said. "Ye're crowdin' on too much sail. But come to think of it, I've heard wuss ideas. Maybe I'll slip across to one of they bars and git a bottle of wine. Enough to muzzy the Johnny's head a bit. I wants you youngers to quiet down. Ye're hoppin' about like a pair of waterfleas. Anybody who see'd ye'd guess there was some'at up. Git yerselves in hand, lads. This here's no pirate game we're at. It's serious work — man's work, ye understand?"

Somewhat abashed, the two boys nodded their heads and when Jonathan left they went back to work, cleaning the hold and decks and trying to control their excitement and pretend to be engaged only in dull ship's labor.

Jonathan was back in an hour carrying a wrapped bottle in one hand and a long gray envelope in the other.

The boys met him as he came over the gunwale.

"It's the way I had it figured," he told them. "This here's the verdict from that Frenchy court. Took it to the agent to read for me. Says I was teetotal in the wrong, and no excuses. Says I ought to lose me master's ticket, and the Frenchies is sending a copy off to the harbormaster in St. John's. That way I guess Barnes figures to git me in deep water with the authorities at home, so they'll never believe me yarn that the ship was robbed away from me. Well, we'll see to all that in good time, so we will. Right now we don't want to give the Frenchies, nor Barnes, nor his Yankee friends, no cause to git suspicious of we. They've set the date for the law case agin us for Wednesday. With the inquiry gone agin me, they be pretty certain they'll win their court case. But I don't aim to let 'em know that I knows it too. You lads keep busy about the ship, like you expect everything to turn out all right. I'm goin' to swaller me pride and go and beg Barnes to help me some, pretendin' I figure to fight and win the case."

It was an interminable afternoon for Peter and Kye. The verdict of the investigation was now known to everyone in St. Pierre and there were scores of idlers who came along to see the ship and speculate on her fate. The Chief of Gendarmes also came aboard. He seemed very casual, but he asked the two boys several pointed questions about the work they were doing. Apparently satisfied that all was in order, he left again after a word with the gendarme guard.

"I think he's fooled," Peter whispered to Kye. "If anyone suspected what we was up to, the police would be sure to put more guards aboard."

Peter was half right . . . but half wrong. Since the Chief of Gendarmes personally suspected nothing, the idea of mounting additional guards had not crossed his mind. But he was not as well informed as some of the other residents. On an island as small as St. Pierre it is difficult to keep anything secret for long. After Paddy Mathews returned to his vessel on the slipway at the shipyards, he had taken his mate and two seamen into his confidence so that together they could effectively plan their part in the affair. All three were honest fellows, but a little incautious. During the afternoon they visited one of the waterfront bars in order to prepare themselves for the night's work ahead. After several drinks one of them, assuming perhaps that the Frenchmen in the bar knew no English, made a joking remark about the surprise Captain Smith would be in for next morning, "when the party was all over." It was only a small slip, but the sharp-eared bartender caught it, and a few minutes later a note was being delivered to Monsieur Gauthier.

Gauthier and Barnes took the warning seriously.

"Spence might just be fool enough to make a break for it," Barnes mused. "And 'twould be the finest kind of luck for us if he *did* make the try — providin' he never got away with it. That *would* put him into the wrong, right up to his stiff neck."

Dusk began to fall about seven o'clock. Jonathan, who had returned aboard in time for supper, looked at the gold repeater watch which had been passed down in the family for many generations — perhaps from the first Jonathan Spence.

"All right, me sons. Time to git a move on. Go aisy as ye can. Don't make no fuss. Act like ye was just two local lads borrowin' a boat for an evenin' row. When it's full dark and ye comes alongside the schooner, rap once on the hull and I'll go on deck and keep yon Johnny-darm busy whilst ye moors to the bow. Off ye goes, now. I figures ye'll do fine."

Doing their best to appear aimless, Peter and Kye ambled down the dock. The few people they passed did not even give them a glance. Reaching the dockyard, the boys looked nervously about and, seeing no one watching, quickly vaulted the board fence. The yard was deserted at that hour except for Paddy Mathews's crew aboard their ship, hauled out on the slip. Hurrying to the water's edge they pulled in the mooring line of one of the skiffs and then, to their horror, discovered that the oars were not aboard.

"What'll we do?" muttered Kye in an agony of frustration. "Can't row with our hands, and we dassn't go back to *Black Joke* for oars."

Peter thought rapidly.

"Stay where ye're to," he whispered. "I'll slip over to Mr. Mathews's boat. I'll tell him what we're up to, and borrow a pair of oars." With that Peter vanished, running swiftly.

He was back in a surprisingly short length of time with the oars tucked under his arms. Kye had already freed the boat, and, as Peter jumped aboard, Kye slipped the oars between the tholepins and began to row.

They did not hurry now, but half drifted out into the harbor. They could see *Black Joke* at the government wharf, looking very peaceful. The street along the shore seemed deserted except for one or two Basque fishermen. Keeping well off shore they rowed the skiff slowly toward *Black Joke*.

Once they saw the guard on deck stand up, stretch himself and cast a casual glance along the docks before settling himself more comfortably against the main hatch cover. He did not glance out toward the harbor at all.

The darkness was deepening rapidly by now and cautiously Kye turned the skiff toward the schooner. A few moments later she had bumped gently alongside the forepeak and Peter rapped on the hull with the handle of his oar.

The two boys heard Jonathan clumping up the companion stairs and thumping across the deck. Then they heard his rough voice as he began talking to the uncomprehending gendarme.

"Pretty dry work for ye, Monsoor," he was saying. "Ye like a little drink? Drink, ye know — glub-glub-glub . . . ?"

In the skiff the boys could imagine him holding the bottle up to his lips, pretending to drink. There was a short burst of French from the guard, but by this time the boys were concentrating on their job. Swarming up the bobchains, Peter soon had the skiff's painter made fast to the schooner's bitts while Kye was making the other end of the line fast to the stern of the skiff. In a moment all was secure. Both boys slipped quietly over onto the dock and then, whistling and with their hands in their pockets, they sauntered along to re-board the schooner amidships. The guard and Jonathan were still standing together. Jonathan nodded his head briefly at the boys and said, "Bedtime, young 'uns, off ye go."

The guard, with the cork already out of the bottle, half-raised it to the lads in salute, then took a long pull.

A few minutes later Jonathan followed Peter and Kye into the forepeak. "Well done, me b'ys," he said. "It's gittin' on for eight bells. All we can do now is wait till we hears from Paddy's lads."

"I spoke to Mr. Mathews at the shipyard, Father," Peter said. "Had to, 'cause there wasn't no oars in the skiff. He give me a pair and said to tell ye he'd be startin' his party behind the Customs House a little short o' midnight."

"Fair enough, lad. Now then, settle yerselves and make out to have a rest. Likely we'll need all the wakefulness we can git afore we're through this night."

It was a miserable business, trying to rest with ears straining for every sound from the nearby streets. The boys could hear bursts of song from the bars along the *Place*. Once they heard the gendarme walk aft, and they thought they noted a stumbling sound to his footsteps. They hoped so, at any rate. The minutes slipped painfully by. Jonathan was actually sleeping, snoring slightly, for he had long ago learned to sleep when he could. But at 11:30 he sat bolt upright in his bunk, wide awake again.

"Gittin' on fer time now," he said. "I'll slip open the companion hatch — I greased it with pork fat after supper — and have a look around."

"Everythin' dead quiet," he reported a few moments later. "Near as I can tell the Johnnydarm's poundin' his ear. Street lamps burnin' bright, and not a soul to be seen."

He had hardly spoken when there was a hoarse shout from somewhere on the docks. It was followed at once by a chorus of rowdy voices singing a famous Newfoundland song called "The Ryans and the Pittmans."

At the first sound, the boys had leapt out of their bunks and crowded around Jonathan at the foot of the ladder.

"That'll be they. Stand ready now, me sons," Jonathan said tensely.

The singing seemed to be coming closer. Then gradually it died down and was replaced by the sound of three or four men's voices beginning to sound quarrelsome. The sound of argument got louder and sharper and was punctuated suddenly by a yell and some sharp cursing. The three in the forepeak could make out some of the words.

". . . Avast, ye sculpin . . . no need to kill a man to make it sound good . . . ," someone was shouting.

By now the argument ashore had turned into what sounded like a full-scale fight, and there was enough noise to waken the town — but still there was no sign of life from the gendarme.

"The seacow must've gone dead asleep," muttered Jonathan angrily. "Well, there's nothin' for it. I'll have to roust him out meself. Come up quick now when I gives the signal," and with that he was gone up the ladder.

The gendarme was indeed sound asleep and snoring happily, the empty wine bottle at his side. Jonathan seized him by the arm and shook him savagely.

"Wake up, ye lead-swinger," he cried. "They's a ruddy war on at the Customs House. War! Fight! Bang — bang! Git over there and break it up!"

Waking suddenly, the poor gendarme was completely at a loss. He did not understand a word Jonathan was yelling at him, but he did recognize the sound of authority in the voice. Staggering sleepily to his feet, he found himself half pushed, half led to the gunwale of the ship, where he became aware of the sounds of mayhem and riot from the back of the Customs shed. He had not yet begun to think clearly, and still half-dazed he started at a run toward the sound, quite forgetting his primary mission of guard upon the schooner.

"Now!" Jonathan whispered sharply down the companionway. Instantly Peter and Kye swarmed up on deck. Leaping to the dock Peter began throwing off the mooring lines while the other two jumped into the skiff, where Jonathan had already flung the spare pair of oars from *Black Joke*'s own dory stored on deck. The man and the boy were soon pulling for all they were worth, while Peter, having cast off the last line, dashed aft and took the wheel.

For two or three terrible minutes, nothing seemed to happen. The two in the skiff were pulling their hearts out, but the schooner seemed anchored to the bottom of the harbor. Peter had put the wheel hard over and was anxiously watching the mooring bollards on the dock, expecting to see them start slipping past him. From the Customs shed the sound of battle still shattered the quietness of the sleeping town. Now that the fake riot had served its purpose, Jonathan and the boys wished desperately that Mathews and his men would quiet down before they woke the whole of St. Pierre to a realization of what was going on aboard *Black Joke*.

But almost imperceptibly *Black Joke* was moving. Inch by inch, her head began to swing out from the quay. Peter felt a slight pressure on the wheel, and the dock began to move slowly away from him. The sweat was coursing down Jonathan's back by then, and Kye was groaning with the effort of hauling on the heavy oars. Neither dared slack off. Gradually *Black Joke* began to gather way until she was slipping silently through the black waters of the harbor. Five minutes — ten minutes — and she had reached and entered the tidal stream that was now flowing out the harbor entrance at a good three knots. On deck, Peter could see the street lights receding, and he began to breathe deeply again. But suddenly he caught his breath in horror.

Although *Black Joke* was being swept out to sea at about three knots, she was not really under control — for the two in the skiff, though they were doing their utmost, could not put steerageway on her. Now Peter saw that the schooner was being swept almost broadside into the narrow channel between the two concrete piers which constituted the harbor entrance. Though he could not see the piers themselves, but only the pierhead lights placed to guide ships at night, he realized that *Black Joke* must inevitably strike one of the piers unless she could be straightened around. Frantically he spun the wheel hard over; but the schooner did not answer. She was still driving broadside toward the invisible but solid concrete wall.

There was no one Peter could look to for help. There was no time to try to get Jonathan out of the skiff. *Black Joke* could strike within two or three minutes unless something was done at once. Half-sobbing with the tension, Peter made his decision. Leaving the wheel he ran headlong for the engine-room companion and plunged down it. The engine had been primed and readied by Jonathan, and now the boy prayed he would have the strength to swing the big wheel hard enough so that the cylinder would fire on the first try. He knew there would be no time for a second try. Crouching, he grasped the handle and, putting every ounce of energy he possessed into the effort, he straightened up. The big wheel moved slowly, there was a smothered cough from the engine, then silence. Desperately Peter completed the turn. *Whoomp-whoomp-whoomp,* went the engine and began to run. Instantly Peter throttled it back to half-speed and leapt for the deck and the steering wheel. He felt the ship begin to gather way and slowly straighten out so as to head down the channel. The pier was now so close he could see the ragged line of rocks below the concrete wall. *Black Joke* was clearing it — just barely clearing. Not more than ten feet separated her from a collision which would have stove in her side and finished her.

Peter had not had time to think of the two in the boat. Caught off guard when the engine started, they barely avoided being run down. The skiff had come crashing back against the ship as she forged ahead, and both Kye and Jonathan had had to jump for it, hauling themselves aboard over the gunwale, abandoning the swamped skiff to its fate.

Once aboard, Jonathan ran aft.

"Good lad," he said to Peter as he took the wheel from him. "Ye've saved our bacon proper. Half-an-hour's run down the buoyed channel now and we'll be in open water; and on a night as black as this, nobody'll catch us then."

Still shaking from the narrowness of the escape, Peter moved forward to join Kye on lookout in the bow. Forging ahead at three knots on her engine and with a three-knot tide to help, *Black Joke* was actually moving past the land at a full six knots. The channel buoys, flashing white to port and red to starboard, were sliding quickly by. Not far ahead, the revolving beacon on Little Pierre Rock marked the end of the channel and the beginning of the open sea.

Looking astern, Jonathan could see no sign of pursuit, or even of an alarm having been given. St. Pierre still seemed to be sleeping soundly as the darkened schooner drew rapidly away.

It was keen-eyed Kye who saw the shadow first. Grasping Peter's arm he pointed off to starboard. "Look there," he said sharply. "Somethin' lying' in the channel — looks like a boat."

Peter had barely seen the dim shape and was just opening his mouth to call a warning to Jonathan, when he and Kye were blinded by an intense light shining full in their eyes.

At the same time, the roar of big engines bursting into life came to their ears.

Jonathan immediately guessed what had happened. Someone had given them away, or else the authorities

had suspected all along that *Black Joke* would try to make a break for it, and now a boat was lying full in their path to intercept them.

A stentorian voice, bellowing through a megaphone, cut across the waters.

"The game's up, Spence. Cut off your engine. We're coming alongside!"

Jonathan recognized the voice as that of Captain Smith and a great surge of rage boiled through him.

Although dazzled by the searchlight, he guessed that the blockading motorboat could not be more than fifty feet or so off the starboard bow. He thought rapidly. If he tried to make a run for it, he would have to haul away to port, and Smith would be expecting just such a maneuver, and be ready to counter it. Well, he thought, they tried to steal my boat because I hauled away last time. *This* time, by the Lard, I'll fool 'em. Whereupon he spun the wheel hard down to starboard, while at the same time yelling to Peter, who had run aft, to open up the old engine to full power.

Black Joke seemed to know this was her final chance. She swung so sharply to starboard that Kye, in the eyes of the ship, almost lost his balance. He staggered back to his feet in time to hear Jonathan's bellow.

"Heave over yer mooring lines to starboard, every line that's loose; HEAVE 'EM ALL OVER, KYE!"

The men on the rum-runner had been caught completely off guard as *Black Joke* came charging down upon them. Motors roared as they attempted to back their vessel clear, but, before they could get underway, *Black Joke*'s bow had struck the motor vessel in almost the same place where she had been struck — by accident — three days earlier. But *this* time she struck as if she meant it! In the darkness, the resultant confusion was monumental. The searchlight on top of the motorboat's cabin top went out as it was smashed by *Black Joke*'s bowsprit. The sound of breaking wood, and the squeal as the two ships slid along each other, was earsplitting.

Doing as he had been told, though without understanding the reason for it, Kye was meanwhile busily heaving overboard every coil of rope he could find. Some of the rope fell on the rum-runner's decks, further confusing things there, but much of it fell into the water alongside her and was sucked toward her churning propellers. This was what Jonathan had intended. He knew that a few turns of heavy line around the rum-runner's propeller shafts would jam them, leaving her to drift helplessly while *Black Joke* escaped.

"*Stop engine, Peter!*" Jonathan bellowed, as the two boats began to sheer apart. *Black Joke*'s own propeller eased to a stop until her headway could carry her clear of the rum-runner and clear of the danger of fouling her own screw.

At this intant the darkness was broken by a stream of orange tracer and the simultaneous chatter of a tommy gun being fired from the rum-runner. The heavy slugs thudded into *Black Joke*'s planking with a sickening sound.

"*Start up agin, START UP!*" Jonathan yelled urgently, and at once Peter spun the flywheel over. Being hot, the engine caught easily, and *Black Joke* went plunging away down the channel, an invisible target now, and running hard for freedom.

Behind her the crew of the rum-runner was in wild confusion. Their boat had suffered considerable damage, though it was mostly superficial. Her decks were a shambles of bent stanchions, hanks of rope, and debris. One of her two propellers was hopelessly fouled with trailing lines, and for a few moments she steamed in circles while her cursing skipper struggled to get her under control.

Nevertheless, only five or six minutes elapsed before the motor vessel was again under way. On one engine, and much hampered by the trailing twisted ropes, she could only make ten knots now, but this was still much faster than *Black Joke* could manage.

Deprived of her searchlight, the rum-runner had to take up the pursuit rather cautiously, but Jonathan, at the wheel of his schooner, soon picked up the sound of her engine and knew that his attempt to completely disable the motorboat had failed.

Although the entrance to the channel was still a quarter of a mile away, there was one final gamble Jonathan could take. If he veered out of the channel now, the rum-runner might carry straight on and miss him in the darkness. It was a dreadful risk, for if *Black Joke* were to strike one of the uncharted rocks outside the channel at her present speed, the bottom would be ripped clean out of her.

"Well, b'y," Jonathan thought to himself, "ye'll lose her anyway if they chaps catches up to ye. Better let her die an honest death." And with that he again put the wheel hard over, this time swinging the ship to port.

"Cut loose the lashings on the dory, Kye!" he called. "Peter, ye git up here on deck! We may strike at any moment, and there'll be precious little time to leave her, if we do. Come on, old girl, keep yer keel off bottom for a while, and you and us'll all be free agin!"

Black Joke had barely sheered out of the channel when there was a roar as the motor vessel shot by across her stern. Had the rum-runners been looking to port they could hardly have avoided seeing *Black Joke* as a darker shadow in the night, but they were staring straight ahead, confident they would overtake the schooner before she cleared the channel entrance.

"Made it, by Harry, made it now!" breathed Jonathan to himself as he eased his vessel off to starboard again, clinging as close to the channel as he dared.

They were almost free. The light from Little Pierre Rock was almost abeam of them, though they were on the wrong side of it. Another hundred yards. . . .

A shudder ran through the schooner. She seemed to groan aloud. The way came off her so fast that it threw both boys to their knees. Her bow rose well up out of the water as she slid forward a few more feet . . . and stopped.

8

The High and Lonely Rock

IT SEEMED miraculous that the ship was still alive; but instead of striking a rock as Jonathan had feared she might, she had run onto an underwater spoil-bank consisting mainly of soft mud and gravel which had been dredged from the channel.

Apparently she was not damaged, but she was so hard aground that Jonathan realized at once she would never come off without a tow. He also realized that his battle to save her was over — and that he had lost.

As soon as she struck he had run to sound her bilges, then, having found she was not making water, he had returned aft, where he stood leaning on the rail, staring into the black night, with the muted roar of the searching rum-runner sounding distantly in his ears. He remained there for some time while Peter and Kye stood quietly behind him, not knowing what to say.

At length Jonathan straightened, then turned toward them.

"Well, b'ys, we tried. Ship, man, and b'ys — we tried. That'll be somethin' to remember, now we've lost her. There's nought left but to wait till they fellers comes and hauls her off — and takes her and we'uns back to port. I figure it'll be prison for me, but I doubt even they Frenchies would chuck a couple of b'ys into jail. Ye must nip around to Paddy Mathews, smart as ye can. He'll take care of ye and see ye git safe home to Ship Hole. I don't rightly know how things'll turn out, but ye're to tell Sylvia I'll be along afore too many days. They Frenchies'll find me a hard cod to hold — that I promise. . . ."

"But why let them catch us at all, Father?" Peter interrupted. "We still has the dory, and they fellers in the motorboat don't know where we're to. We could be ashore in an hour, and then let 'em find us if they can."

"The Johnnydarms would find us soon enough, lad," Jonathan answered kindly. "St. Peter's is a mighty small island, ye understand, and we with no friends to hide us, and not a word of the language either. They'd take us pretty quick. . . . But hold hard a moment . . . mayhaps they wouldn't. I'd clean forgot about Colombier — Colombier Rock. She's not more'n an hour's pull from here. Six hundred feet high and so steep-to it'd take a mountain goat to climb the cliffs. I've heard tell there's a ten-acre field on top, level as yer hand, with a pond in her full of fresh water. Pierre Roulett, he used to talk about the Rock — claimed he was the only feller what knew his way around her. Told me 'twas full of puffins and rats. The puffins come in from the sea to nest in the cliffs, and the rats was washed ashore from some wrecked ship a long time back. I doubt anyone would ever think to look for us there. When they comes aboard the schooner and finds the dory gone, they'll more'n likely figure we're pulling for Fortune, trustin' to luck and darkness to git clear. *Let* 'em think that, then! By the Lard Harry, 'tis just what we'll do — only we won't try for Fortune tonight, for they'd be sure to spot us and take us at dawn. We'll row to Colombier and hide till there comes a fog — and that won't be long, not in these waters. *Then* we can make for Fortune. By that time they Frenchies'll have give up lookin' for we. With a bit of luck and not too much stiff weather, we can make safe harbor in ten or fifteen hours even if we ain't lucky enough to git picked up by a schooner partway over."

The old accustomed strength had returned to Jonathan's voice as he talked, and it infected the two boys so that they threw off their depression and entered excitedly into the new plan.

"What-all will we take along of us, sorr?" Kye asked.

"The sleepin' gear, lad. The cookin' pots. All the grub ye can lay yer hands to. Bring along yer kitbags — there's plenty room in our big dory. And Peter, ye nip down and heave up the spare jib for to make a tent out of. It'll make a boat sail later on when we sets out for Fortune. Hop to it now, me sons; that prowlin' sea-wolf might happen to blunder into us afore too long."

Heedless of the difficulties of getting around the decks in the pitch-darkness — they did not dare show a light — the boys rushed off to collect the gear, while Jonathan rigged the slings on the dory and shoved her clear of the rails for launching. Twenty minutes later she was in the water and fully laden. The boys were already aboard her, waiting for Jonathan to join them.

Jonathan delayed a few more minutes. Silently he walked *Black Joke*'s deserted deck, seeing nothing, but knowing from old familiarity every aspect of her. Standing finally at her wheel he patted the worn spokes affectionately.

"Good-by to ye, girl," he said softly. "Ye've done fine by me ever since ye was launched. Now I've done ill by ye. But if ever there comes the chance — someday — I'll git ye back."

He turned to the rail and quickly climbed down into the dory where, without a word, he took up a pair of oars and began to row away from his ship.

There was only one set of oars, for the second set had been lost when the borrowed skiff was smashed against *Black Joke*'s side at the harbor entrance. But Jonathan was a husky man, and in a few minutes the dory was well away from the abandoned vessel.

It was too dark to take bearings, so Jonathan rowed by the sound of the ocean swells breaking on the unseen shore of St. Pierre. Keeping the sound on his port side he pulled steadily while the boys sat silently at either end of the dory. There was nothing much to say. They were aware of how great a pain the parting from his ship had brought into Jonathan's heart, but they were buoyed up by the exciting possibilities which lay ahead.

After an hour the sound of breakers to port grew faint.

"We's off the end of St. Peter's now," Jonathan said abruptly. "Colombier lies pretty nigh a mile to seaward. Keep yer ears liftin', lads, and tell me when ye hears surf ahead of us."

"I can hear the rum-runner, Father," Peter replied. "Sounds like he's gone back toward the channel. Hope he misses it and hits a rock."

"They'll be a rare mad crew aboard of her, anyways," Kye said. "Give her a good knock, we did. I don't reckon they'll think too kindly of us; figurin' we got clean away, ship and all."

"They'll find the ship soon enough," Jonathan interjected shortly. "And I'll thank ye lads to leave off talkin' about her now."

The boys subsided into listening silence until at last Kye thought he could hear the distant sound of surf ahead. Jonathan pulled the dory in the direction Kye indicated. The sound grew stronger, and after another ten minutes the dory was hovering on the back swell from breakers that were bursting, still unseen, against the foot of the sea-cliffs of Colombier.

"We don't dare try landin' till we gits a little light," Jonathan said. "But we'll pull round to the seaward side so there's no chance of being spotted from the land when first light comes."

Dawn was not far away. A pearl-gray lightening of the eastern horizon showed its progress. The loom of the great rock began to emerge and harden into a distinct and forbidding shape: a sheer-sided mountain rising from the sea. Flights of puffins began to plane down from the ledges of the cliffs, skimming the dory as they headed off for the day's fishing.

It was already half-light when Jonathan, after a searching examination of the cliffs, chose a landing place in a narrow cleft just wide enough to admit the dory. There was no proper place to haul her up, and so the boys and the man had to unload her bit by bit as she surged up and down against the rocks. It was tricky work, for the rocks were wet with slime. Once Peter slipped and plunged into the deep water at the cliff-foot, but Jonathan instantly grabbed him by the slack of his jacket and hauled him back to safety.

When the gear was landed all three of them turned to the job of sliding the empty dory up on a sloping face of spray-washed rock. She was heavy, and there was no purchase for their feet, but somehow they managed to get her out, and overturned her. Jonathan lashed her to the rocks with several lengths of rope.

" 'Twon't hold her if a real sea comes up," he said, "but 'tis the best we can do. Now then, me b'ys, make up a back-pack for each of ye — not too heavy, mind — and we'll tackle the cliffs. What we can't carry now we'll come back for later when we gits the chance."

By this time it was full daylight, with the sun just showing to the east. The cliffs no longer looked quite so formidable and, seen from the bottom, they were not absolutely sheer. The many ledges were thick-covered with deep moss which was riddled by the burrows of rats and puffins.

Having started the two boys up the cliff, Jonathan remained behind to scuff a small avalanche of moss down over the dory, effectively concealing it from any but the closest inspection. Then he too shouldered a pack and began climbing upward.

Peter led the way, scrambling from ledge to ledge; pausing now and again to search for the best route, but gradually gaining height. A hundred feet up he found a narrow ravine that slanted sideways up the cliff, so that the going became easier. All the same, it took half an hour of hard climbing before the three of them were at the top.

Before them they beheld a saucer-shaped plateau about three or four hundred yards across and covered with luxuriant mosses. Right in the middle was a small pond of ice-clear water with a jumble of split boulders along one side of it.

"Pretty near made to order for a camp," said Jonathan, when he had caught his breath again. The boys clearly agreed, for without a word they heaved off their packs and, running to the edge of the pond, sprawled belly-down in order to drink deeply.

Jonathan did not join them. Making his way to the southern edge of the little plateau, he sat down on the moss and stared out across the St. Pierre Roads. Two miles away, and standing out clearly, was *Black Joke*. She was no longer alone. The rum-runner was lying close off her stern and Jonathan could see men scurrying about his own vessel's decks. While he watched, they passed a heavy towing line between the two ships, and a few minutes later a whirl of white water showed at the motorboat's stern as she strained to haul *Black Joke* clear. Jonathan could hardly bear to watch; yet he could not tear himself away. He did not notice that the two boys had joined him.

"She's comin' off, Father," Peter said softly.

Jonathan did not reply. He stared intently as the little ship he loved so well began to move stern-first back into the channel. In a little while the towing rope was cast off. The men who had boarded the schooner had evidently managed to start her engine. Slowly, sadly, *Black Joke* turned and began moving toward the harbor of St. Pierre.

Jonathan got to his feet and turned his back on the sight.

"That be the end of it," he said shortly. "All right, me b'ys, let's git us a camp set up amongst they boulders. Then we'll have grub, and catch some rest. Nothing to do now until the fog comes in."

"Shouldn't we have a sentry?" Kye asked a little diffidently. "The rum-runner ain't goin' back to harbor. Looks to me like she's goin' to have a right good search around for us."

"Good idea, lad," Jonathan replied. "I'll take first watch. Two hours on for each of us. Peter, ye'll be next. Best git some sleep now while ye can."

It did not take long to get the camp set up. The spare jib was stretched between three massive boulders and firmly anchored with stones, to form a comfortable shelter. The gear was piled inside in case of rain — though rain looked unlikely, for the morning was clear and bright. Kye meantime got some grub ready. They did not dare risk a fire since the smoke might give them away, but there was plenty of cold boiled pork and sea-biscuits, washed down with water from the pond.

During Jonathan's watch he saw nothing to alarm him. The motor vessel moved out to sea on a course for Fortune, obviously hoping to find the dory. It was soon out of sight, far beyond the three-mile limit. The law don't seem to mean nothin' to they chaps, Jonathan thought indignantly. They'd pick us up right out of Newfoundland waters if they got the chance. Powerful anxious to git their hands on me, I guess. He chuckled. Can't say I blame them overmuch. Must have hurt more'n their dignity when I rammed them in the channel.

At ten o'clock he woke Peter and went to sleep himself. Peter made the circuit of the high plateau but saw nothing except a number of St. Pierre fishing dories puttering by under the lee of the great cliffs. Becoming a little bored with the quietness, Peter explored part of the cliff-face in search of puffin nests. He found scores of them, and after breaking an egg or two to see if they were fresh, he collected three or four dozen and brought them triumphantly back to camp to show Kye when he woke him for his watch.

"You're right smart, you are," said Kye, when Peter showed him the eggs and bragged about the fine omelette they would make. "How you goin' to make an omelette when we dasn't light a fire? Goin' to eat your omelette raw?"

Peter was crestfallen. "Well," he said defensively, "if we was to git marooned on this here island, I guess we'd be glad to eat raw eggs."

The idea of being marooned stayed in Kye's mind as he wandered about the plateau peering out to sea occasionally. He knew that the dory was in a most unsafe position, and he also knew it was impossible to haul her far enough up the cliffs to make her secure. Born to the sea, he was quick to recognize the signs of weather. Now he began anxiously to scan the northwestern sky where thin bands of diffuse white clouds were appearing. A breeze seemed to be making up from the north too. Kye began to worry. The signs were those of a nor'westerly blow.

Not waiting to finish his watch, he decided to wake Jonathan. Jonathan took one look at the sky and immediately roused Peter. "Trouble comin', b'ys," he said. "There's a blow on its way. And the dory's layin' on the weather side of the rock, right where the seas will come ashore."

"What'll we do, then?" Peter asked.

"Have to try and bring her round to the lee side," said Jonathan, "but it's risky with all them fishin' boats about, and the rum-runner bound to come back this way afore too long. We'll hang on a bit, Mayhaps the blow'll not amount to much. Can't ever be sure with a nor'-wester."

They waited tensely for an hour to two while the wind rose slowly but surely, and a sharp chop began to build on the face of the ocean far below.

"Can't leave it no longer, lads," Jonathan said at last. "We'll have to git her off that shore afore she gits broke up. I'll take her round myself. One feller in a dory won't look so bad if we gits spotted, but three of we would be a dead give-away. Peter, you come down and help me launch her. Kye, you keep a watch on the back-side of the island and if ye sees a boat comin' close, heave over a stone so's it'll hit the water somewhere's nigh me and give me a warnin'. Come on, Peter, there be no time to lose."

Half falling and half scrambling, the two of them went over the edge and down the cliff. After a considerable struggle, they managed to right the dory. She slid eas-ily enough into the water, for the breaking seas were already half floating her. Jonathan made a wild jump to get aboard and in a moment was rowing strongly to draw clear of the rocks. Looking down from the top of Colom-bier, he had not realized just how big the sea had be-come, and now he was having all he could do to keep the dory under control.

Peter began climbing up again, for there was no fore-shore which would have enabled him to walk around the island at sea-level. In order to meet Jonathan and help him haul the dory up again, he would have to climb all the way up to the plateau and then descend the other side. Meanwhile Kye had run to the lee side of the plateau and was searching the narrow gap of water be-tween Colombier and St. Pierre. There were no French dories in sight. Evidently the fishermen had read the

weather signs too and had run for shelter while they could.

Seen from above, Jonathan's little boat seemed like a minute chip being tossed in a spring freshet. First one end, then the other, seemed to be pointing straight up at the windswept sky. Jonathan was standing up in order to get more leverage and was leaning into the oars with the fury of desperation as wind and seas did their best to drive him onto the rocks at the foot of the northern cliff. He realized now that he had badly miscalculated the force of the storm, but there was nothing he could do about it except strain every muscle and hope he could get safely around the corner of the island, run down the eastern side, and then pull into shelter on the southern side.

He was very close to exhaustion by the time he was clear of the hungry rocks. Then he was able to let the wind take the dory and she began to drive rapidly past the east coast of Colombier, pushed by both wind and waves. Jonathan rested, slumped over the oars. But in a few minutes the dory had blown to the southeast corner, and once again he had to take up the oars and pull with all his strength in order to gain the promised shelter.

Watching anxiously from above, the boys saw him take a strain on the oars. Then they saw him suddenly lose his balance and fall backwards, full-length into the bottom of the dory.

"An oar broke, an oar broke!" Peter yelled at the top of his voice. "He'll never make it now, Kye! He'll blow ashore on St. Pierre! We got to do somethin' quick!"

"Nothin' we *can* do," Kye yelled back over the whine of the wind. "Why don't he git up? What's the matter with him? He ain't movin' at all! Must have hit his head on the for'ard thwart. Must have knocked himself clean out!"

"He'll be drowned," Peter wailed.

"No he won't," cried Kye, though he was far from sure. "Ain't no sea ever made what could overturn a dory. He'll drift down the harbor. Somebody's *bound* to see the dory down there. They're bound to see it come ashore. Somebody'll help him. Most likely he'll come-to anyway afore she hits the beach. He'll be all right, Peter, ye hear me? He'll come through all right!"

Jonathan had struck his head a savage blow and now lay totally unconscious in the bottom of the boat. But a dory is the most seaworthy small craft ever invented, and as Kye had said, there was no danger of it overturning. Wind, seas, and the inflowing tide were carrying it rapidly off to the southeast, almost directly toward the entrance to St. Pierre Roads. If it continued to drift in the same direction, it would eventually fetch up near the relatively smooth beach where many of the St. Pierre fishermen hauled out their own dories. But Kye was wrong about one thing; Jonathan was not likely to recover consciousness for a long time. The sharp edge of the birch thwart had nearly split his skull, and he was suffering from what would later prove to be a serious concussion of the brain.

From the high, windswept plateau, the two boys

watched until the dory vanished from their sight behind the southwest headlands of St. Pierre. They continued to lie watching for some time afterwards, hoping against hope for some sign that Jonathan would survive. They saw nothing until they spotted the returning rum-runner driving hard for harbor, and rolling and pitching in a manner which showed she was having all she could do to keep on her course.

Peter jumped to his feet and almost danced with relief.

"They'll spot the dory, Kye," he shouted. "Can't miss seein' it. They're bound to pick him up. He'll be all right now. He's sure to be."

It was only when their fears for Jonathan's safety were somewhat alleviated that a realization of their own plight began to dawn on the boys. They were marooned on Colombier.

The wind was now so strong it was hard to stand against it, so they made their way back to the sheltered hollow where the tent was flapping like a wild thing. Having added more stones around the edges to hold it down, they crawled inside and began to discuss their plight.

"What ye reckon we ought to do, Peter?" Kye asked.

"Stay put, I guess. Don't have no choice till this blow is over. Then we could signal one of the French dorymen aisy enough and git took off."

"We better not do that," replied Kye. "Jonathan might have his own plans for us. Maybe he'll try and git word to Skipper Mathews for him to pick us off when he's outward bound for Newfoundland. And if he decides that ain't no good, he'll tell the Frenchies where we are and they'll send off a boat for us. I figure we ought to just bide aisy and leave it up to he."

"Guess you're right, Kye. We got grub and a snug camp and they ain't no use lookin' for trouble afore we has to. After what we done, I kind of think the Frenchies would put us in jail if we was only six-year-olds. And another thing, there ought to be other Newfoundland schooners comin' in here and we could maybe signal one, if Skipper Mathews can't help out."

Although still worried about Jonathan, the boys' spirits were rising rapidly at the prospect of being marooned on the gigantic rock and having to live like Robinson Crusoes. They mightily enjoyed their first night in the homemade tent, listening to the howl of the wind overhead and the steady rumble of the big seas breaking at the foot of the cliffs. Morning brought some second thoughts, however, for the gale continued unabated and the supply of cooked food was running low. By mid-afternoon they were looking speculatively at the puffins' eggs, and before noon of the following day they had concluded that raw puffins' eggs might be edible after all. They were. Downing the first one raw was the hardest part, but Peter tried the experiment, and when he found he could keep it down, he managed to eat half a dozen more. Kye followed his example.

On the afternoon of their third day on the rock, the wind dropped light and the seas began to fall off. But though they spent several hours watching the mouth of

St. Pierre's harbor, they saw no sign of any boat setting out to rescue them. By evening, when the seas had smoothed down considerably, a stream of power dories began to put out, filled with fishermen — but none of them paid any attention to Colombier. Some of them puttered past within a few yards of the shore rocks, but their crews did not even glance up toward the high crests where the boys lay watching.

Life on the island was becoming tedious. The boys had explored the crest very thoroughly, but exploration of the cliffs was not something one would tackle for fun, for a drop of six hundred feet to the shore rocks was not a pleasant prospect. Their diet of cold water, raw eggs, sea-biscuits, and the occasional handful of brown sugar was beginning to sour. Worse still, the rats on the island, which normally lived on the cliff-face eating puffins' eggs and young puffins, had discovered the camp. During the third night the rats staged an invasion of the tent in search of food, and the boys spent most of the night leaping about and striking at the scuttling creatures with rocks or bits of stick. Although the rats were not dangerous, they made sleep impossible.

As the fourth day dawned, the boys found that the pleasures of being marooned had worn pretty thin. They were hungry, tired, bored, and beginning to feel lost and lonely. They could no longer even begin to guess at what was happening on St. Pierre. Only one fact seemed certain, that for some reasons of his own Jonathan had not told the authorities where they were. Presumably this meant he had made arrangements for their rescue by Mathews, or some other friendly person — but the uncertainty was beginning to tell on their nerves. There was always the thought, suppressed as much as possible, but ever-present in the back of their minds, that Jonathan might *not* have made it safely to St. Pierre. It was a black thought, and one they would not face, yet it hovered always near.

Towards noon on the fourth day they were lying to-gether on the south crest looking at the mounded heights of St. Pierre lying less than a mile off. They were in a dark and gloomy mood as they watched a fishing dory coming toward the channel between the two islands, from the direction of Miquelon lying to the north.

It was a big dory, brilliantly painted in sky-blue with red trim, and it was coming along at a fast clip. The lads could see only two figures aboard it, one of them a burly man sitting on the engine-cover and wearing a beret, while a youth with red hair was in the stern steer-ing.

"Maybe we ought to signal that one," Peter said tenta-tively. "We can't stay stuck up here forever. I'm sick of eatin' puffins' eggs and chasin' rats. We got to find out what's happened to me father, and we can't find out nothin' here."

"Quit your grumblin'," Kye replied shortly, "We agreed to stick it out till we got word from your dad. If we don't hear nothin' before tomorrow night, it'll be time to start thinkin' about givin' up. Lessen ye're ready to quit, of course!"

"Spences don't quit!" Peter replied hotly. "And I don't

aim to be the first. Let that dory go along. I'll wait as long as you can."

Kye suddenly grasped Peter's shoulder. "It ain't *goin'* along," he said, excitement mounting in his voice. "It's turnin' in! I believe it's goin' to land right on Colombier!"

9

The Basques Take Sides

THE BOYS watched anxiously as the big dory turned sharply toward the cliffs. Although it appeared to have come from the wrong direction, they still hoped it might have been sent to fetch them, for why else would a dory land on Colombier? Peter was feverishly anxious to hear news of his father, and so, jumping to his feet he began to yell and wave his arms, though his voice could not have been heard above the sound of the dory's motor. Kye grabbed him and pulled him back from the edge of the cliff.

"Take it easy," Kye said sharply. "We don't know for sure it was sent for we. Let's wait and see what happens afore we sticks out our necks."

The dory engine stopped and the boat drifted toward the rocks. At the last minute the man with the beret leapt ashore, caught the dory's nose and fended her off. The redheaded boy joined him, bringing with him two big wicker baskets. After mooring the boat, man and boy slipped the baskets over their arms and began to climb the steep cliffs.

Kye and Peter were puzzled. "What do ye guess them baskets is for?" Peter asked. Kye shook his head. "Keep yer eyes peeled till we find out; but don't let 'em see us yet."

The man and the boy had now separated and were working their way up the cliffs by two different routes. When they were about halfway up, they reached the area where the puffins nested and they were soon surrounded by clouds of the little birds.

Peter was watching them intently.

"They didn't come for us, at all," he said at last. "They're after eggs. What'll we do now? We better figure what we're going to do."

Retreating to their camp, the two boys conferred. Peter was for making contact with the strangers at once, on the grounds that he and Kye could not remain on Colombier much longer in any case. But Kye was still doubtful of the wisdom of such a move. They were arguing heatedly about it when a sound of boots on rocks brought them to their feet.

Coming up behind their tent, after having evidently scaled the cliff to the rear as they were arguing, was the boy from the dory. They could not avoid him nor escape. They could only stand and wait to see what he would do.

The strange lad with the red hair seemed immensely surprised. He stared at the tent for some time, then at Peter and Kye. Finally he spoke.

"*Qui êtes-vous?*" he asked.

Peter and Kye stared back at him uncomprehendingly, whereupon he ran to the edge of the plateau and began shouting. Two or three minutes later the head and shoulders of the man emerged into view. He was a big, burly fellow with a hawklike nose, dark eyes, and a mass of black curly hair slipping out from under his beret.

He took one astounded look at the scene, hauled himself up on the level ground, and came striding forward.

"By Gar," he cried in a booming voice. "You fellows don't come from St. Pierre, eh? Who you are an' how you get up here?"

Peter said the first thing that came into his head.

"We been shipwrecked, sorr," he quavered.

"Shipwreck? Where the ship what wrecked, hey? I don' see no ship. Don' hear about none either! I theenk maybe you *garçons* come out of the sea like mermaids, or maybe you come out of the sky? What you theenk, Jacques? You theenk mebbe we catch two angels?"

The red-haired boy grinned.

"*Mais non, mon père,* they don't look much like angels. . . . Too dirty in the face."

By this time the fisherman had reached the camp and was standing looking down at the boys and their gear. He too was smiling, and Peter and Kye's fears began to wear off.

"Guess we better tell the truth," Peter said sheepishly. "Me name's Peter Spence, sorr, and this here's

Kye Spence. We belongs to Ship Hole over to Newfoundland . . ."

"Spence? Spence?" the big man interrupted. "Maybe
you the sons of Johnny Spence, *non?*"

"Yiss sorr, that's it. Jonathan Spence, he's me father,
and Kent Spence he's Kye's father, only he's dead now."

The fisherman gave a bellow.

"By Gar! Kent, he ees dead? A good man, that one.
And Johnny, whereabouts that old devil got to anyhow?
They *both* good fren's to me. Long time I don' see or
hear of them."

"Would you be Mr. Roulett, sorr?" Kye asked hes-
itantly.

"Pierre Roulett, that's me. And thees my son,
Jacques. He speak the Engleesh more bettair than me;
got education in the school. Now we all sit down, I
theenk, and you two fellows tell me what go on."

In their relief and excitement, Peter and Kye tried to
tell their story all at once, but Pierre managed to calm
them down and eventually get the facts. When they had
finished, he looked grave.

"*Sacré bleu!* Johnny Spence got himself beeg trouble,
eh? Me and Jacques, we been for the lobster fishing on
Langlade. Got plenty lobster too. We go to St. Pierre
for sell them, but first we theenk we get some eggs.
Now we got more'n eggs. *Bien!* We got to theenk a
leetle." He got out a short-stemmed pipe, filled it, lit
up, and sat puffing hard for a few minutes.

"I tell you what we do," he said at last. "Johnny, he
my very good fren' and I do most anything for him and

for hees *garçons* too. I theenk best thing Jacques and I go on to St. Pierre, so we fin' out what happen to Johnny and hees boat. Maybe I get to talk with heem. Then he and I make the plan. *Demain* — tomorrow — I tell everyone I go fish for cod on Plate Bank, but I come here instead and tell you what happen.

"Jacques! *Allez!* To the boat. Bring up meat, some bread, some cheese. Look like theese boy, they eat nothin' but sea pigeon eggs . . . and maybe some rats too, eh?"

Jacques did not seem to mind the long climb down and back, but went off cheerfully while Pierre, who never seemed to stop talking, continued to question the boys about their adventures.

"That *capitain* Smith, he ees one tough fellow, I don' like heem and he don' like me. I theenk maybe Meester Barnes he work with Jean Gauthier — the beegest robbair evair live on St. Pierre; I got no use for him neither. But I fin' out everything, you bet. I got more fren's in St. Pierre than anyone. I hear everything I want to know."

At last Jacques arrived back. He was sweating profusely but still smiling, and obviously enjoying the novelty of discovering two strange boys on the crest of Colombier.

"Here is the food, my father," he said in his best English.

"*Bon!* Now we eat a leetle. Then we go. Tomorrow we come back. You two sleep good. You got nuthin' to worry about now. Me, Pierre Roulett, I tell you that!

Capitain Smith and Meester Barnes and that *diable,* Gauthier, bettair they start to watch out for themselves!"

Rather stunned by the ebullience of the big fisherman, Peter and Kye made no attempt to answer, but tucked into the proffered food with ravenous appetites. When the meal was finished, Pierre shook them both by the hand, nearly shaking the hands right off them, and said good-by. In a few moments he and his son were on their way down the cliff. The two boys watched the dory until it was out of sight around the corner of St. Pierre Island.

Rats or no rats, Peter and Kye slept well that night, knowing they had found friends at last.

It was late afternoon of the following day before they heard the putter of an approaching boat. They met the Roulett dory — named the *Frontenac* — on the narrow foreshore, but Pierre would tell them nothing until all four had climbed the cliffs, laden with food, and had eaten a full meal.

"Now I tell you what marches," he said when they had finished. "Some of eet ees not so good, but you are not leetle babies, so I don' make the easy talk — I tell you straight, *non?*"

The story he had to tell was grim. Jonathan had indeed been picked up by the rum-runners, but he had been unconscious at the time and had remained unconscious through the three succeeding days. He was still in the St. Pierre hospital — under arrest, and under guard. Pierre had spoken to one of the hospital doctors

— an old acquaintance — who had explained that Jonathan was suffering from a severe concussion. He would recover; but it would be several days before he was fit to leave the hospital.

"And when he leave," Pierre said, "he go straight into the calaboose — what you call the jail. I hear from another fren' of me that they make the charge of steal the boat — steal hees *own* boat . . . and he sure to get two months unless he kin pay the fine. It don' be no leetle fine either. Those officials, they plenty mad weeth him, you bet!"

Even Pierre had not been able to get in to see Jonathan, but he had smuggled in a note to say that the boys were safe, and that he, Pierre, was taking charge of them for the time being.

"That way, he won' worry none. He know for sure Pierre Roulett the bes' man for to take care of trouble in whole of St. Pierre and Miquelon."

Pierre's next move had been to find out what had happened to *Black Joke*. Through a cousin who worked for Gauthier, he had picked up some information; and through other sources he had acquired enough more, so that he could guess the story in its general outlines.

"That fellow Barnes, he worked with Gauthier all right like the hand work in the glove. Day after Smith bring in *Black Joke*, they have the lawsuit in the *Palais de Justice*. Quick and sweet, that one. They fin' Johnny make the mistake in the channel and Smith, hees boat hurt for twenty thousand francs damages. So they say Johnny got to pay. But, say the President, Monsieur

Spence he got no money, so we sell hees boat to the highest biddar so we can pay Monsieur Smith.

"Very next day, they have the auction. Only two fellows make the bids. Monsieur Gauthier and a fellow he hire to bid 'longside heem. And Gauthier, he get the boat for twenty-five thousand francs — one thousand dollars! They *steal* that boat from Johnny.

"Very nex' day they put *Black Joke* on the slipways. They tell everyone they goin' to feex her up for to carry salt fish from Newfoundland to Trinidad and they got the carpenters right to work changin' 'round her hold. But one of those carpenters he ees my sister husban', and he tell me they feex her up for to carry *le whiskey* underneath the fish. An' he tell me they got a great beeg engine in the warehouse for to put into her. Hundred and fifteen horsepower diesel; enough for to power a boat twice as beeg as *Black Joke*.

"I go all over. I listen and I ask the question, and now I tell you what I theenk. I theenk they use that boat of Johnny for to go straight to United States with *le whiskey*. I theenk they try to fool the revenue fellows — make them theenk she only slow leetle old fishing boat. Maybe it work too . ... unless we stop them. An' once that boat gone from St. Pierre, maybe we nevair see her no more.

"I ask what happen to the two boys was on *Black Joke*, but nobody wan' to talk about that. They theenk you two got kill when the rum-runner open fire with machine gun, or get drownded after maybe. And even the officials, they plenty scare about that. They afraid maybe comes a beeg stink from Newfoundland if the word get out. Barnes and Gauthier, they don' be veree happy about it, because eef the Government of *Terre Neuve* start to ask the question about you *garçons,* maybe the whole cat come out of the bag, eh?

"Me, I don' tell nobody that you is safe — 'cept Johnny. Bettair keep them fellows scare so much as we can. So now I make to hide you good. We stay here 'till it get dark, then we go off in *Frontenac* to Miquelon. That's the place where I was born. That's where I live mos' of my life, and that's where I take my wife to live. She fine Newfoundland girl, that one, with beeg blue eyes and the red hair, but *sacré bleu,* what a tempair that woman got! Eh, Jacques?"

Jacques had taken no part in the conversation so far. It was difficult for *anyone* else to talk when Pierre was talking, but now he answered the direct question.

"Maybe she needs the hot temper with you, my father," he said, grinning.

"*Nom de nom!*" shouted Pierre. "What for you say that? I theenk I beat your head in with one of theese dead rats the boys have kill!"

He made a lunge for his son, but Jacques skipped neatly out of the way and, in the mock chase which followed, all three boys were soon overcome with laughter, for Pierre was a natural comedian, and his wild lunges and rugby tackles after his son were always wide of the mark. Finally he grew winded, and trotted back to the camp site.

"Ah well, I settle hees hash some other time. Now

then, you *garçons* listen close to me. I take you to Miquelon, that's where all the people my frens. They don' like the people in St. Pierre, they don' like most of the Yankee rum-runners, an' they don' like Monsieur Gauthier. They hide you good, an' look after you good. Jacques, he stay with you in Miquelon for to speak the French for you and keep you out of the trouble. Me, I come back to St. Pierre and see what I can see. Okay?"

"Thank 'ee, sorr," said Peter, "but Kye and me, we can't just sit still and let me father stay in jail, nor let them rum-runners steal our ship away neither."

Pierre struck his forehead with his fist and rolled his eyes.

"What you theenk? You theenk I let Johnny stay in jail, an' let the robbairs sail away with *Black Joke?* But first we have to make the plan, you understan'? And while we do that, you stay still in Miquelon."

So it was arranged. For the rest of the afternoon Peter and Kye listened wide-eyed to Pierre's stories of fishing, of shipwreck, of smuggling, and of the rum-runners. He had an inexhaustible fund of yarns, and the lads were hardly aware of the passage of time. But suddenly it was growing dusk. Pierre jumped to his feet and, spouting orders like an admiral, soon had them at work packing the camp and toting the gear back down the cliffs to where *Frontenac* lay moored. Shortly after dark she was loaded and they cast off.

The boys had never before been in one of the French sea-going dories and they were fascinated by her. Her hull was similar in shape to the small dories used in

Newfoundland, but she was almost three times as big. She was powered by a seven-horse motor amidships, and when it was run wide open she could do nine knots.

"Beeg motor for fish boat, eh?" Pierre asked. "Well, we don' fish *all* the time, you understan'? Sometime we got business across in Newfoundland for take the grub to the poor peoples and bring back some other stuff. Times like that we maybe have to go pretty fast, when the *Terre Neuve* coastguard cutter he come sniffin' after us."

Even at nine knots the trip to Pierre's home took more than three hours, for the isolated little fishing village of Miquelon lay at the extreme northern tip of the large island of Miquelon, which was itself the northernmost of the three French islands. Only about four hundred people lived in the village, and they were almost all of Basque descent. The Basques came originally from the border areas of France and Spain and they are amongst the world's most independent and stubborn people. For a long time the Basque fishermen on Miquelon had regularly supplied passing ships with contraband but, when the great new smuggling trade with the United States sprang up, the St. Pierre merchants tried to organize the whole of it through their own hands. The Basques resisted fiercely and their big dories continued to go to sea to meet passing boats and to supply them. They also supplied a number of the professional rum-runners as well, since Miquelon was so isolated that it was almost impossible for a spy to go there without being detected, and shipments out of

Miquelon could not be traced by the United States government agents in St. Pierre.

The two boys learned all this, and much more, about Miquelon during the journey. By the time Pierre turned the bow of the boat toward the dark and unseen shore, they were full of curiosity to see the place. But their curiosity had to wait until morning, for the village was asleep when they arrived, and they saw little of it as they followed Jacques and Pierre along the single narrow street to stop at last at the Roulett house.

Mrs. Roulett got out of bed to let them in and as soon as she realized that they were also Newfoundlanders she almost smothered them with attention. It turned out that she had come from an outport not far from Ship Hole, and she was so full of questions that the boys could hardly manage to answer them all. It was some time before even Pierre could get in a few words, and tell the story of the Spences and of *Black Joke*. When she heard what had happened, Mrs. Roulett displayed her famous temper.

"Why them maggoty dogfish!" she shouted. "Let me lay my hands to *Mister* Barnes, or Gauthier, or that Yankee captain, and I'll make salt fish out of them or know the reason why! Ye got to do something about this, Pierre. Ye *better* do something, or I'll claw *your* ears into the bargain!"

"Hey there, *ma petite!*" cried Pierre, trying to stem the flow. "Slow down that engine or you burn out the bearing! Don' you worry. We feex those fellows before we finish or my name not Pierre Roulett. Right now you bettair make the bed for these *pauvre garçons* before they go soun' asleep at the kitchen table."

In an instant Mrs. Roulett's temper cooled.

"Ye poor lads," she crooned. "What must ye think of me, keeping ye awake while I talk my head off. Come now, ye'll have the bed that was for Jacques and it's long past time ye was in it."

Twenty minutes later, having been tucked in — which they hated — Kye and Peter were alone in a big bed under the eaves of the two-story wooden house.

"Ye still awake, Peter?" Kye whispered.

"Yep."

"Quit worryin' then. Jonathan will be all right. I got a hunch this Pierre can do just about as much as he says he can — and that's a lot."

"I hopes so, Kye. One way or t'other, we got to git me father free."

10

The Men of Miquelon

IN THE MORNING the boys explored Miquelon under the guidance of Jacques. The village consisted of a long line of weather-beaten wooden houses set a little way back from a deeply curved gravel beach where the thirty or forty local dories were hauled up when not in use. There was no harbor, only the open roadside of Miquelon Bay where large vessels could not anchor safely for long. Although fishing was the main occupation, Jacques explained that the local people had also formed a sort of smugglers' co-operative. Working as a group, they would order a cargo of liquor from Europe which would be brought to Miquelon by some old tramp freighter. Recently a shipload of whiskey had arrived off Miquelon, on consignment to American owners. The Basques had agreed to handle this cargo, taking it ashore for storage, and then loading it on the American rum-runners as it was required. They were not aware of the fact that this was part of the new plan of which *Black Joke* and several other re-fitted and re-engined schooners were to be the vital elements.

The two boys were the subject of much interest as Jacques took them about. Before long they had a following of a score of small children and as many dogs.

"Not many strangers come to Miquelon," Jacques explained, "so everyone is curious about you. But you don't need to worry. If you are a friend of the Rouletts, you are a friend to everyone here and nobody would think to give you up to those people at St. Pierre."

He led the way down to the great curved beach and Peter and Kye had a good look at the dory fleet. The big boats looked a little bit like Italian gondolas, for each one had a small square "house" amidships, and both ends of the dories were curved up steeply into an abrupt sheer.

"They are the best seaboats in the world," said Jacques with pardonable pride. "With these dories we fish thirty miles to seaward of the islands. Maybe you like to make a fishing trip in one of them?"

"Sometime I'd like to," Peter replied. "Only not now I guess. Not till we git me father out of jail."

"You must have patience, Peter," said Jacques. "It will not be tomorrow he is free. But he *will* be free. If my *père* says so, it will be so. Now it is better for you, I think, if you don't worry about it."

"That's what *I* been tellin' him," Kye interjected.

"Come, then. We go see my Uncle Paul. He is the great fisherman. I will ask him to take us to the Banks tomorrow."

Meanwhile Pierre had been talking with the other leading men of the settlement. It was agreed that the Spence boys should stay in Miquelon and that no one outside the settlement would be told of their presence there. Pierre himself was to go back immediately to St. Pierre with a load of fresh fish. The fish were to ensure that his trip did not arouse any suspicion, and when he had worked out some plan to help Jonathan Spence he would send a message to the village and the local people would help in any way they could.

Pierre's boat was soon loaded with cod that had been brought in that morning by other fishermen, and after a quick good-by to the boys and to his own family he set off for St. Pierre, accompanied by a friend named Pascal.

On arriving at St. Pierre, well before noon, Pierre delivered his fish and went on into town. It did not take him long to find out that Jonathan was much better and would probably be discharged in a few days, but would then have to stand trial for attempting to steal the schooner. Pierre at once sent him another note:

Boys is safe my home Miquelon. Everybody here still think they dead and is better they think so. Tell them you don't remember about what happen because the knock on the head make you forget everything. Leave all to me. I send message your wife telling all well and not worry okay? Better you eat this paper — P.

His next stop was the shipyard, where he found it

impossible to gain entry. Two dockyard workers were lounging about the entrance gates, and when he tried to pass them he was stopped.

"Pardon, Pierre," one of them explained. "It seems there has been some stealing from the yard, and the boss says no one comes in now without permission from him."

Pierre made no attempt to get permission. He guessed at once that the guards were really there to prevent spies from discovering what was being done to *Black Joke*. In any event he did not need to go in. At twelve o'clock he was loitering near the gate when his cousin, the carpenter, came out on his way home for lunch. The two walked side by side up the narrow streets.

"They move quickly," his cousin told him. "Last night they bring the new engine aboard with much secrecy. Only the Yankee sailors are allowed on board now, and nobody is supposed to know what's really going on. Everybody working in the yard got twenty dollars to keep his mouth shut except to say the schooner is being repaired after the damage in the collisions."

"Good, good," said Pierre. "They try to fool the American agents, eh? But they don't fool us. Now you must watch close. I want to know when they are ready to launch the ship. Leave a message for me at the Basque Café."

The Basque Café was Pierre's next stop. He had some lunch and then idled away a few hours chatting with other Miquelon fishermen, for this was their favorite spot when in St. Pierre. At four o'clock Pierre's friend, who worked for Gauthier, pushed through the door, saw Pierre and nodded briefly, then went to the bar for a drink of Pernod. After a few minutes he casually sat down at Pierre's small table.

"Gauthier is worried," he said quietly. "He and Barnes are afraid about the business of the two boys being shot or drowned. The shooting was an accident — one of Smith's men lost his head. But they think if the matter comes to the attention of the British authorities in Newfoundland, they will demand an investigation and the Governor here will not be able to refuse. Much might come to light which they wish to keep hidden. So far it does not seem that Monsieur Spence remembers what happens. But he may recall it at any time and if he can get a message to Newfoundland, there may be trouble. Gauthier wants to get the schooner out of here as soon as possible. She will sail with a cargo of salt cod supposed to be bound for Barbados, but instead she will go to Miquelon and dump most of her cod and take on whiskey. After that she will sail for the United States. That is the plan, I think, but it is difficult for me to be sure. I do not hear all that goes on, you understand."

"You hear enough, my friend," Pierre said warmly. "Now let us have another Pernod and talk about the weather. It is not wise even here to speak too much of secret things."

Despite their worries about Jonathan and *Black Joke*, Kye and Peter were having a good time in Miquelon. After showing them through the village, Jacques took them off in a small dory to try for some lobsters. They rowed for half a mile along the beach until they reached an outcrop of rocks. Here the water was calm and extremely clear. Jacques produced a wooden box about a foot square and three feet long, open at one end and closed at the other with a pane of thick glass.

"Hold the glass part under the surface, Kye," he instructed, "and look down through it. Then you will see everything on the sea floor. Watch out for the lobster. He will be backed into the holes in the rocks with just his feelers poking out."

Kye did as he was told and found he could see every detail of the bottom. Crabs moved slowly over the few open places between the rocks, and small schools of young cod wavered back and forth. But no lobster did he see.

"How about a peek?" Peter asked impatiently. "Bet you I can spot a lobster even if you can't."

Reluctantly Kye handed over the water glass. Jacques sculled the dory slowly over the rocky area. Suddenly Peter gave a shout. "There's one!" he cried. "Saw his big old claw for a minute till he hauled it in."

Now Jacques picked up a fifteen-foot pole which had been lying in the bottom of the dory. Attached to one end was a cluster of big hooks. Leaning out over the side of the boat he lowered the pole very slowly while

Peter held the glass so Jacques could see through it.

"You are right, Peter. A big fellow too, but wise I think. Kye, please, will you take some handfuls of cod flesh out of the can in the bow? Let it sink in the water where the lobster is."

Kye did as he was told and the bits of cod spiraled down through the clear water to litter the bottom near the lobster's lair.

"He can smell underwater you see," Jacques explained. "When he smell the good food, he will come out perhaps."

All three heads were crowded over the water glass, watching expectantly. Twelve feet below them they could see the feelers of the lobster waving in the current as he "smelled" the water. Then very cautiously he began to move, walking on his underbody legs, with his great claws stretched menacingly out before him. Jacques held the hooked end of the pole about three feet above the lobster, being careful to keep it as still as possible. As the lobster reached the first shred of codfish, Jacques gently lowered the tip of the pole until it filled the entrance of the lobster's lair. The crustacean seemed to sense that something was wrong. He gave one powerful flick of his tail and shot backwards. Jacques gave a sharp jerk on the pole.

"Ha, ha, my friend. Got you!" he cried. Rapidly hauling up the pole, he flicked the end of it in over the boat. The lobster had been only lightly hooked and he fell free, rattling onto the floorboards at Peter's bare feet and instantly spreading his claws for defense or attack.

Peter hopped nimbly out of the way.

"It's a monster!" he cried. "Never see 'em that big t'home, does we, Kye?"

"That is because you fish differently for them in *Terre Neuve*," Jacques explained. "There you use the lobster pots; but the big lobsters, they will not go in the pots. You must catch them this way."

Leaving the big fellow to scuttle about the floorboards the boys sculled slowly on. By noon they had caught three more lobsters. They were content as they rowed home and presented their catch to Mrs. Roulett.

Lunch was something of a surprise. Neither Peter nor Kye had ever eaten French cooking before, but Mrs. Roulett had become an expert at it since marrying Pierre and moving to Miquelon. The boys picked away rather tentatively at the main course which seemed to be a roll of some kind of white meat stuffed with an indescribable substance. Peter finally plucked up courage to ask what it was.

"Stuffed squid, me b'ys, stuffed squid!" said Mrs. Roulett, beaming proudly.

Kye went white, his eyes took on a glassy look, and he hurriedly covered his mouth with his hand as if expecting the worst to happen.

Mrs. Roulett burst into a gale of laughter.

"Never fret, Kye. Don't think of *what* it is, just think of how good it *tastes!* And take a mouthful of wine, if your stomach's feelin' queer."

Peter and Kye had noticed glasses of red wine standing by their plates, but had assumed the presence of the wine was a mistake. The idea of drinking wine with meals had never occurred to them. But Kye was desperate. He snatched up his glass and took a great swallow and instantly forgot about the squid, for the wine was dry and bitter and made him gag. He was up and away from the table like a shot, and when he came back some time later, pale-faced and weak, he was only able to grin feebly as he apologized.

"Never mind, Kye," said Mrs. Roulett. "Tonight I'll give ye a good Newfoundland feed of fish and brewis. I guess you'll have to get on to Frenchy cookin' slowlike."

"I'll starve first," muttered Kye under his breath to Peter.

In the afternoon Jacques took them duck hunting on a huge salt-water lagoon which lay to the south of the village. They had only one gun between them, a double-barreled 12-gauge hammer-lock which belonged to Pierre. Each boy took his turn hiding in the salt grass near the edge of the lagoon while the other two made a wide circle inland and, having reached the lagoon again, walked back on either side of it toward the hidden gunner. Flocks of teal got up from the brackish water and went whistling down the pond. Between them they killed five teal.

"That is enough," said Jacques, when they had retrieved the last bird. "We will give some to my Uncle Paul when we ask him to take us fishing, and the rest *ma mère* will cook for us to eat in the dory tomorrow. It is not good to kill more than one needs."

Toward evening they arrived back at Miquelon, tired, hot, and hungry; and, as she had promised, Mrs. Roulett fed them fish and brewis. The wineglasses again stood by their plates, but neither Peter nor Kye touched them.

"It is all right, you know," Jacques said. "Here everyone drinks the wine with the meals. But it is only half-wine, you understand; the rest is water."

"I'll take me water straight, thank'ee," said Kye feelingly.

When the meal was over and the dishes washed, Jacques took the boys to see his Uncle Paul, a gray-bearded man in his sixties who lived alone in a house at the very end of the beach. Paul could speak no English but he shook the Spence boys warmly by the hand, and when Jacques asked him if they could go fishing with him in the morning he nodded his head and replied with a spate of French.

"He says he is glad if we come," Jacques translated. "It is lonely on the Banks, and his partner is sick. We will meet him on the beach three or fours hours before dawn."

It was pitch-dark when the three boys reached the beach the following morning. There was still no moon, and a light southerly breeze was blowing. Uncle Paul was waiting for them.

Once the boat was floating, all four jumped aboard and pushed it off into deeper water. Then Uncle Paul lowered the propeller shaft, for the Miquelon dories are built with a hinged shaft so that the propeller can be lifted into a box or "well" in the hull in order to protect it from being damaged when the dory is hauled ashore.

The engine caught as Uncle Paul spun the flywheel, and they were away. By the time the eastern sky had begun to grow light, the breeze had become stronger. By dawn it was blowing fresh, and the dory was so far at sea that the mountains of Miquelon Island could hardly be seen at all. To make matters worse, the fog was coming in from the southeast.

Peter and Kye began to feel a little uneasy. They did not mind being at sea in a schooner, but this open dory was something else again. The only cheerful thing was the presence of half a dozen other dories scattered around the horizon on every side.

Uncle Paul shouted something to Jacques who scrambled to the bow and pushed the anchor overboard.

They had arrived over the offshore banks where the cod congregate.

Now Uncle Paul gave each boy a jigging reel and then he opened a wooden drum and with his hand shoveled out a mess of revolting-looking objects.

"They are clams, for bait," Jacques explained. "Now we fish, eh? Bait your jiggers and we see what we can catch."

Slipping a clam on one of the gang hooks, each boy began to lower his jigger. Though they were over a "bank" the water was still nearly twenty fathoms, or one hundred and twenty feet deep. When they felt the jigger hit bottom, they hauled in about a yard of line and then began jigging the bait up and down.

The fog swept over them, and the rest of the dories vanished. Suddenly Paul began hauling in his line, hand over hand. There was a swirl of water and over the gunwale came a twenty-pound cod. Uncle Paul flicked the line sharply, and the jigger came out of the big fish's mouth.

The boys did not have time to admire his catch. They were "into the fish," as Newfoundlanders say, and within a few minutes each of them was hauling in a cod.

Uncle Paul grinned and shouted something at them.

"He says you are bring good luck," Jacques translated. "Big fish today, and plenty fish too — hoy!" He paused as a tug on his line made him hurriedly begin hauling in.

It was not new work for Peter and Kye, for they had often jigged cod before, but never under quite these circumstances. After the first few minutes, it ceased to be fun and became hard work. Each of them was catching a fish every three of four minutes, and the effort involved in hauling in the big cod was backbreaking. The fish-well or fishhold in the middle of the boat was soon carpeted with cod.

From somewhere astern came the thudding of a motor, whereupon Paul took a hitch in his line, then picked up a big conch shell and blew a penetrating blast. The sound of the motor grew stronger and Paul

continued to blow at intervals till suddenly the bow of
another dory loomed through the fog not twenty feet
away. Its motor stopped and it drifted slowly closer,
revealing three more of the Basque fishermen.

"Hello, Paul," one of the newcomers shouted. "Lots

of fish, eh? What you think about the weather? Looks dirty, maybe?"

Jacques translated this — it had been shouted in French of course — and went on translating the conversation for the benefit of the Spence boys.

"Going to blow up strong, all right," Uncle Paul replied. "We fish another half-hour only, then we run for shelter."

They fished the remaining half-hour, by which time all three boys' arms were aching so that they could hardly lift them. Then Jacques hauled up the anchor and they got under way for home.

They had not realized how big the sea had become until they started to run before it. The great gray rollers came up behind them, caught the dory, and lifted her stern until she seemed to point her nose straight to the bottom. But Uncle Paul, at the tiller, did not even notice. The Spence boys hung onto the gunwales for dear life and wished they had *Black Joke* under them.

With wind and sea astern, the run home was much faster than the outward journey. As the wind whined harder, the fog began to shred away and the mountains of Miquelon came into view, growing larger every minute. Hunger was beginning to gnaw at the boys' stomachs and they were delighted when Uncle Paul opened the grub box. He tossed each of then a cold roast duck and a great chunk of bread, then he hauled out a wine bottle and offered it to each in turn. There appeared to be nothing else to drink aboard the dory, but even though they were extremely thirsty Peter and Kye shook their heads in refusal.

"Guess ye got to be born a Frenchy to drink that stuff," said Peter.

"Born crazy, more likely," Kye replied and closed his eyes at the memory of his previous experience.

The lighthouse on the northern tip of Miquelon was in sight now, standing high and white against the rocks. The little boat drove on, pitching wildly as it changed course to round the bend of the island, then they were in the lee of the land, and the sea died away. Half an hour later the dory was nosing in to the gravel beach.

Winching the dory up the beach was hard work too, but there was still more work to be done before the day ended. Eight or nine hundred pounds of cod had to be forked into baskets and carried to the nearby splitting tables. Then each fish had to be gutted, its head removed, and the remainder neatly split. The boys worked as hard as Paul, for it was work they knew well, but it was not until nearly dusk that the last split cod was carried to the brine barrels.

There was no question of staying up late *that* evening. Hardly was supper finished when all three boys went off wearily to bed. It had been a hard day but a good one, and they had been so busy that they had had little time to think of Jonathan and of *Black Joke*.

11

Pierre Plots a Rescue

ALTHOUGH the boys had been able to put *Black Joke* out of mind for a little while, the fate of the schooner was occupying Pierre Roulett's thoughts almost exclusively.

To tell the truth, Pierre was thoroughly enjoying himself. There was a good deal of buccaneering instinct in him, as there is in most seafaring Basques, and the prospect of organizing a plot to seize a ship did not daunt him in the least.

In the evening he had taken his friend Pascal for a walk up the mountain behind St. Pierre where they could be alone and unobserved. As they sat watching the lights come on in the town below them, they could also see *Black Joke* sitting in the slip.

"Tomorrow morning she is being launched," Pierre explained. "She will remain in the harbor for a few days to complete her re-fit and to take on a cargo of salt cod for Barbados. That is what her clearance papers will say, at any rate. She will sail with Smith as Captain, and four or five of his Yankee friends for crew, but she will not go to Barbados. She will go instead to Miquelon where she will unload most of her fish and take on one thousand cases of whiskey. This she will do at night. Smith intends to take her right in to our little wharf and load from there. This will save him much time, for loading from the dories at sea is slow work. It will save time, but it is also dangerous unless the weather is very calm, for there is no shelter at our wharf. Therefore, Smith will not sail until he is sure of calm weather at Miquelon. He will take with him a pilot who can show him the way to the wharf in darkness and, by happy coincidence, that pilot is my second cousin, Gabby Morazi, whom you know. Captain Smith will load his whiskey and depart well before dawn so that he can be out of sight of the islands by daylight. When he departs he will still have Gabby aboard to pilot him clear of the shoals in Miquelon Bay.

"We can make no move while the schooner is at the wharf. The people of Miquelon are our friends and relatives, but they are also businessmen, no? They would not take kindly to the idea if we tried to seize the schooner there, for it would be bad for future business with the rum-runners. Therefore we shall not try.

"But this is what we *shall* do. When Gabby pilots the schooner out of the bay he will bring her to a certain spot, and there the Yankee sailor handling the lead line will suddenly find shoal water and will give the alarm. Gabby will order the engine stopped while he tries to locate himself. And then, my friend, two dories will appear out of the darkness astern and Gabby will hail them. He will tell Smith they are fishermen friends of his bound for the offshore banks; and he will ask the Captain for permission to consult them so that he can get the schooner back in the proper channel. The dories will come alongside, and before the good Captain Smith — who will have no reason to suspect fishermen — has time to draw his breath, or his pistol, there will be eight men standing on the deck of his ship, all carrying shotguns. Even though it will still be far too dark to shoot at a duck it will not be too dark to shoot at a man, as the good Captain and his crew will quickly realize when they note that the shotguns are pointed straight at them. You follow me, yes?"

Pascal chuckled. "You are very clear, Pierre," he said. "I for one will follow you. Let me see now. . . . One thousand cases of whiskey divided between eight men is —"

"Not a thousand," Pierre interrupted. "You do not yet know all my plan. There is still the matter of my friend, Captain Spence, and there is the matter of the ownership of the schooner which was stolen from him. We cannot just give him back the ship, for by law it now belongs to Smith. Also what good is Captain Spence's ship to him when he is still in jail, hey? No, no, my friend, it pains me, but there will not be a thousand cases for us to divide. Eight hundred cases will be given back to Monsieur Gauthier and his American friends, but, *not until Monsieur Spence's fine is paid and he is free, and not until he has in his pocket a bill of sale* which once more makes him the owner of the ship Black Joke."

Pascal looked somewhat crestfallen for a moment. "Ah, well," he said philosophically. "Twenty-five cases each is better than a kick in the behind, is it not so? But tell me Pierre, what shall we do with the ship and the whiskey, and with Captain Smith and his desperados, while we are making the bargain with Gauthier?"

"That is easy, my friend. Captain Smith and his so-tough sailors we will put ashore on the *far* side of Mi-quelon. It should take them ten hours or so to climb the mountains and come down to the village. Our people will then rent them a boat to take them to St. Pierre so that they can deliver our terms to Monsieur Gauthier.

"As for the whiskey, while Smith and his men are mountain climbing we will put it ashore in the sea caves near *Anse du loup* . . . eight hundred cases in one cave, and two hundred in a very secret cave known only to me. When Captain Spence is free and owns his ship again, I suppose we shall have to tell Gauthier where his eight hundred cases lie."

"Maybe we will forget where we put them, eh?" his companion asked hopefully.

"It is possible," replied Pierre solemnly. "There *have* been times in the past when my memory has failed me . . . but no more of that. There are many things to do. Tomorrow morning you will go in my dory to Miquelon and you will speak privately to our friends and you will prepare them for the work ahead. You will have two dories ready, and the shotguns well cleaned. You will watch the weather for a likely day and then wait until I arrive — I shall borrow a dory for the trip from a friend here in St. Pierre. I will leave here well in advance of the schooner, so that there will be ample time for us to reach the shoal in Miquelon Bay before Gabby so kindly brings Captain Smith to meet us. You will also warn the men to say nothing even to their wives — wives have leaky tongues — but you will tell *my* wife, whose tongue is not leaky, but is more like a sharp sword and one she will prick me with if I keep a secret away from her. You may also tell Jacques and the Spence boys, for it is their right to know our plans."

"What about the authorities in St. Pierre, will they not come searching for the schooner?"

"I do not think the authorities will be *asked* to search for us. For one thing, there will be the matter of the schooner's false clearance papers from St. Pierre. For another, there will be the assurance from me that if such a thing is attempted I will send word to Newfoundland that two Newfoundland boys were shot in St. Pierre Roads and that the matter was hushed up with the connivance of the officials of St. Pierre. In addition there will be my promise that none of the whiskey will ever be seen again if a search is started. No, Pascal, I think we will be left alone to settle matters with M. Gauthier and his friends in our own way."

When the boys came down to breakfast the following morning, they found a visitor waiting for them in the big kitchen. It was Pascal, who had arrived from St.

Pierre during the night in Pierre's dory and who had already told Mrs. Roulett the details of Pierre's plan. Now she explained it to the three boys, who sat listening with rapt attention.

"I bet John Phillip, the pirate skipper, never thought up anythin' as smart as that," said Peter admiringly, when Mrs. Roulett had finished.

"Pierre can think straight enough when he wants to," said Mrs. Roulett grudgingly. "Trouble is, he usually don't bother. It does sound like a good plan, but if Pierre gets anyone hurt, I'll take the broom to his behind! Now then, ye b'ys, off with ye and find some mischief, but don't let on a word of what ye've heard."

With the knowledge of Pierre's plan to cheer them up, Peter and Kye had no difficulty filling in the hours. They fished for lobsters again, and one morning they went with Jacques to a stream which flowed down from Miquelon's mountains, and spent half a day catching brook trout. On another occasion they borrowed some of the nondescript dogs that roamed the village and took them hunting rabbits which abounded on the slopes of the island's hills.

Miquelon seemed a veritable paradise to the boys, and the time slipped past quickly even though the weather remained unfavorable to Pierre's plan. For two days there was a brisk onshore breeze which completely precluded the possibility of a schooner landing at the little wharf, and on the third day there was such a heavy fog that no vessel could have found her way into Miquelon Bay. But on the morning of the fourth day the sky was clear, the sea was almost dead calm, and there were no wind clouds to indicate a blow in the offing. All the village dories put to sea early for the fishing banks and the three boys were on the beach to greet them when the boats began to arrive home in the late afternoon. They helped Uncle Paul haul up his dory, and Jacques inquired anxiously about the forthcoming weather.

"It will stay fine for a day, maybe two days now," Uncle Paul replied after a reflective look at the sky. "Why do you ask, eh? Maybe you wish to come fishing with me again?"

"Perhaps," Jacques answered noncommittally. "Come on, Peter and Kye, let us help my uncle with his fish."

Later, at the supper table, the boys and Mrs. Roulett excitedly discussed the possibilities that this night might be *the* night. Pascal came in for a few minutes to report that he and the six picked men were standing by and that two dories had been prepared for quick launching.

"I am sure it will be tonight," he told them. "Pierre said Gauthier was very anxious for the schooner to sail before trouble started over the missing boys, and already she has been lying in St. Pierre nearly a week. Pierre is probably on his way here to tell us that she comes, and to take the lead in what we intend to do. I shall go to the beach now and wait for him there."

It would have been impossible to keep the boys at home, even had she tried to do so, so Mrs. Roulett reluctantly gave them permission to go to the beach too. But she warned them sternly that they were to stay out of "that Pierre's monkey business, and keep clear of the wharf, ye hear me? If they schooner fellers should happen to recognize ye, it would spoil everything."

Darkness fell and Miquelon became very tranquil — to outward appearances at least. But at the far end of the beach, half a mile from the wharf and the center of the village, an observant eye might have distinguished the dim red glow of two or three cigarettes. There, lying at their ease in the rough salt grass beside the beach, were seven men and three boys. They were waiting impatiently for the sound of an approaching dory. But though all of them were straining their hearing, they could not detect the sound they sought.

Early that same afternoon Pierre Roulett had been at work bailing the water out of a dory he had borrowed, when a little boy came seeking him.

"You are wanted at the Basque Café, Monsieur Roulett," he had said.

Pierre had dropped the tin dipper and crossed the *Place* in long strides. As he entered the bar, his quick gaze swept the dim-lit place and hesitated for a second on the face of his friend from Gauthier's office. The friend drooped an eyelid and made an almost imperceptible nod of his head toward the harbor. Pierre paid him no further attention. Ordering a Pernod, he drained it at a gulp and then turned and briskly left the bar. The game had started.

Five minutes later the borrowed dory swung away from the dock and went puttering down the channel with Pierre at the tiller.

Figuring four hours at the maximum to reach Miquelon — for this dory was not as fast as his own — Pierre
reckoned on arriving between eight and nine o'clock.
He guessed that *Black Joke* would not clear from St.
Pierre until shortly before dark, and that she would not
reach Miquelon dock much before midnight. There
would therefore be time enough to arrange to intercept
her at the Miquelon Bay shoals — but not much time
to spare.

Pierre's dory rounded out of the channel and ran
through the passage between the island and Columbier.
As the dory started on the crossing of the broad channel
separating St. Pierre from Langlade, she seemed to be
vibrating more than she should have done and Pierre
carefully checked the single-cylinder engine. It seemed
in perfect order. Nevertheless the vibration of the boat
increased slowly as the miles rolled on and it seemed to
be coming from under the stern. Opening the top of the
well, into which the propeller could be withdrawn for
landings on hard beaches, Pierre peered down into the
turmoil of water being churned up by the propeller.

He drew a sharp breath at what he saw. The propeller shaft was not turning true but was waggling about
like a puppy-dog's tail. And for that there could only be
one explanation — the hinge on the shaft had become
slack. Sooner or later, and probably sooner, the loose
hinge would give way and then the engine could run as
well as it wished without moving the boat another inch.

Pierre sprang forward and throttled the engine back
to dead slow. But this was only prolonging the moment

of crisis. He thought rapidly. There was a sail aboard
the boat, but the weather was so calm that any attempt
to sail the dory would be useless. There were the oars, of
course, but not even a giant could have rowed the big
dory the twenty-five remaining miles to Miquelon in
time to keep the rendezvous with *Black Joke*. Pierre
frantically scanned the surrounding seas for the sight of
another dory that he might hail for a tow. But the fishing dories had all put into port after their day's work,
and the seas were empty. Only one possibility remained
to Pierre and that was to beach the dory and hope, by
some miracle, that he could repair the damage.

Pierre swung the dory's head for shore. He was now
cursing himself bitterly, for, although he had carefully
checked the engine to make sure it was in good order
before leaving St. Pierre, he had taken the condition of
the shaft for granted. It was so seldom that anything
went wrong with the shaft hinges of Miquelon boats that
the possibility of such an accident had never even
crossed his mind.

He recognized the magnitude of the task ahead of
him even before he had driven the dory's bow up on a
convenient stretch of beach and leapt ashore. One man
could never hope to haul out a Miquelon dory by himself, nor turn one over. If he was to repair the shaft at
all, he would have to work under water, and the sea at
this season of the year was still so brutally cold that only
a seal or a fish could stand it for long.

He did not hesitate. Wading in beside the dory he
took a deep breath, ducked under, and felt his way to

the shaft joint. The light was good enough so that he was able to see at once what had gone wrong. Normally the hinge should have consisted of two tubes of brass, each with an end slipped over one section of the shaft, and linked together by a bronze pin to form a sort of universal joint. But in this case someone had substituted a *steel* pin, and the steel had worn away the soft brass fittings to the point where they were now only linked by a shred of metal.

Pierre surfaced, puffing, and already shivering almost uncontrollably. Throwing himself into the boat he searched the spare-parts box for another hinge, but there was none. All he could find were two flat strips of iron and a roll of wire. These, he thought, might just possibly serve. If he could lash the iron strips along the joint, rather as a man would splint a broken arm, he might, just *might* get the boat to Miquelon, or at least to within walking distance of it. But even if the repair job was immediately successful he knew he would have to run the boat dead slow, and it would be touch and go whether he could reach Miquelon in time.

Pierre Roulett was not the man to give up while there was the slightest chance. Grabbing the strips and the wire he prepared to go under the boat again. . . .

On the beach at Miquelon the men and the boys were waiting with growing anxiety and impatience. Eight o'clock passed. Eight-thirty, nine, and still there was no sound of an approaching boat to be heard from the silent ocean. No one spoke. No one expressed the rising doubts that each one felt. Ten o'clock came and went and finally the doubts could be suppressed no longer.

"This cannot be the night, after all," one of the men said, breaking the uneasy silence. "The schooner cannot have sailed, or Pierre would have been here by now."

"Unless something happened to him," one of the other men remarked.

"Something happen to Pierre? Huh! Nothing would stop that one. No, the schooner could not have sailed, that is all. Perhaps some trouble with her new engine. But the weather will be good for a time, and no doubt it will be tomorrow night she comes."

"We will wait here anyway for another hour — just in case," said Pascal. "You are all agreed?"

There was a murmur of assent and then the flare of matches as more cigarettes were lit. The seven men settled back and began talking in low voices amongst themselves of fishing and other matters. But the three boys remained silent. Their disappointment was almost too much to bear after the tensions of the evening. They did not even feel like talking to one another. Finally Kye got up and went wandering along the beach by himself.

He had not gone a hundred yards when he stopped and stared seaward. He could see nothing except the stars reflected on the water close inshore, but his acute hearing had surely detected some sound from seaward, and very faintly, almost as if he were feeling it rather than hearing it, there came to him a rhythmic thumping.

In seconds he was back amongst the group on the beach.

"There's a boat comin' now!" he shouted, forgetting the need for quiet.

Jacques immediately repeated what had been said, in French, and everyone was on his feet. One by one, the others picked up the distant sound.

Peter's heart was beating so hard with excitement that he was almost choking. Then one of the men spoke quietly. It was a second or two before Jacques translated.

"He says it is a boat, but it is not a dory. It is a big engine, a diesel. He thinks it may be the schooner."

"But where is Pierre? Where is Pierre?" cried Peter, and his voice was almost a wail.

No one replied. Slowly, slowly, both Peter and Kye began to realize what the others already understood. Somehow, Pierre Roulett had failed.

It was not for want of trying. At that moment Pierre's dory was still twenty miles from Miquelon. Pierre himself was barely conscious. Prolonged immersion in the icy waters had nearly paralyzed him. Nevertheless he had made some sort of repair, and the dory was under way, though moving slowly. Hazily Pierre calculated the time it would take him to reach Miquelon. Twenty miles — seven hours or more at the dead-slow speed which was all he dared risk. Too late — far too late. He gripped the tiller with a hand which shook as if he had the palsy, and swung the boat back toward the shore. He

was abeam of the Langlade sand dunes, and it was now
possible to walk along the shore to Miquelon Island;
then, by a mountain path, to Miquelon village. Walking would get him there as quickly as if he stayed with
the crippled dory, and furthermore if he did not get
ashore and warm himself soon, he knew he would be
useless when he reached Miquelon in any case. The
dory grated on the shingle and Pierre crawled stiffly over
the bows, hardly able to stand. Setting his teeth he began to walk along the beach, and gradually the blood
began to flow again. Soon he was trotting through the
darkness; but all the time a voice was whispering inside
his head: "Too late. . . . Too late. . . ."

"Even if Pierre comes now, it will be too late," Pascal
was saying softly. The throb of the schooner's engine
was now loud in the night, and she would soon be easing
in to the dock. Her foghorn sounded, two long blasts followed by two short ones.

"That is the signal to the people ashore who look
after the whiskey," Jacques muttered to Peter and Kye.
"It is to wake them so they will harness their pony carts
and be ready to work. It is *Black Joke* that comes, there
can be no doubt."

Peter and Kye felt sick. Everything was suddenly falling apart. *Black Joke* would be lost forever; and with
her would go the only chance of freeing Jonathan from
jail.

"Won't they try the plan anyway?" Peter asked plain-
tively.

"Not without Pierre. No, they will not try," Jacques replied, and scorn was mixed with bitterness in his voice. "Already they have decided to go home. Look, some of them are going now."

It was true enough. Denied Pierre's leadership, the men had decided to give up the attempt. Their shadowy figures began to melt away into the darkness until only the boys and Pascal were left. The man put his hand on Jacques's shoulder, kindly.

"It is no use, Jacques. Without Pierre we can do nothing. I am sorry. It would be best for you three to go home and go to bed. Perhaps in the morning Pierre will come, and perhaps he has made a different plan — a better one. Go on now, go to your home, eh?"

Wordlessly the three boys turned away and began the long walk home. They had not gone far when Peter stopped abruptly and the other two almost fell over him.

"We *got* to do *somethin'*!" he whispered fiercely. "Kye, we *got* to. Why can't we take a dory and try the plan ourselves?"

" 'Twouldn't work, Peter, and ye knows it. Three of us agin five or six rum-runners? And only one shotgun betwixt us? Shake it out of yer mind. It's crazy."

"All right," Peter replied between his teeth. "Ye knows it all. But I tells ye one thing sure, I'm not goin' back to bed while me father's boat sails off for good. I'm goin' to the wharf and I'll figure somethin' out or bust!"

"Ye'll git yourself into a real kettle of fish, that's what ye'll do," replied Kye. "So I guess I'll have to trot along to git ye out of it."

Jacques hesitated for a moment. "I think it will do no good at all," he said at last. "But if you two go, so must I. I am certain my father has had trouble somehow, and now it is up to me to do what I can to help you. But we must be careful. We will stop at our fish store. There are many old clothes there. You two must dress to look like Basques, for even though it will be dark on the wharf, the Yankees might recognize you." And he led off toward the Roulett fish store at a trot.

~~~~~

12

~~~~~

A Desperate Venture

THE FISH store was pitch-dark and smelled strongly of codliver oil and old nets. Jacques cautiously lit a stump of candle and by its flickering light the three fitted themselves out with worn bits of fishermen's gear. With dirty berets pulled firmly down over the sides of their heads, and their faces smeared with "cutch" — the reddish substance used to preserve the nets from rotting — in a dim light all three boys could now pass muster as three slightly built Basque fishermen.

"By the time the schooner docks, the people will have started to haul the whiskey to the wharf on the pony carts," Jacques explained. "There will be no lights on the wharf because they might be seen by one of the *Terre Neuve* customs' cutters that sometimes lie off Miquelon at night hoping to catch one of your schooners with a load of contraband. There will be starlight — enough so that the men can see what they are about, but, if we are careful, no one will notice us."

"We better not go all together in a lump," Peter inter-jected. "Best go one by one."

"I don't see why we're goin' at all," Kye grumbled. "What can we do when we gits there, 'cept pile up trou-ble?"

Peter's blood was up, "How can we *know* what we can do until we sees what's goin' on? We'll mosey round for a bit, then in about a half-hour we'll meet in the churchyard just back of the wharf. By then maybe we'll have some ideas. Anyhow, it's better'n lyin' in bed, waitin' for *Black Joke* to disappear forever."

Kye had no answer to that. "All right," he muttered. "Let's git it over with. I'll go first, I guess."

The other two gave him five minutes start, then Peter followed and, after another interval, Jacques also left the fish store.

It was a dark night, but the blaze of stars gave suffi-cient light so the boys could see that there was already a considerable bustle near the wharf, even though the schooner was not yet in sight. Five or six two-wheeled pony carts were lined up at the foot of the wharf, each cart laden high with whiskey cases. More pony carts were arriving from the direction of the warehouses. There was a good deal of noise. Ponies whinnied shrilly, and men shouted instructions and jokes at one another. Over this local hubbub the throb of the ship's diesel was now plainly audible; and as Peter reached the foot of the wharf and ducked between two pony carts, he saw a black shadow thickening on the water and im-mediately recognized it as the silhouette of *Black Joke*.

A wave of anger and frustration filled him, and forgetting caution he walked straight to the end of the dock where half a dozen men were waiting to take the schooner's lines. No one paid him the slightest heed. The night was full of dim figures moving busily in all directions, and one more attracted no particular attention.

The throb of the diesel ceased, and there was a gentle swish of water as the schooner came alongside. Someone yelled out in English, "Get them bleedin' lines ashore. We ain't got all night!"

The lines had hardly been made fast when the clatter of pony-cart wheels showed that the whiskey was being brought out. Aboard the vessel there was a babel of confused curses and orders as hatch covers came off and as two or three of the schooner's crew began heaving crates of salt cod up on deck.

"Herd some of them Frogs on board," bellowed a voice which Peter recognized, with a sting of fear, as that of Captain Smith. "Put 'em to work for their dough. Get the blankety fish off onto the dock and start that whiskey comin' aboard!"

A looming figure leapt from the ship and caught Peter by the arm.

"Come on, you," a rough voice said. "You heard the Captain. Git across there and start heavin'. *Allez! Allez!*"

Almost before he knew what had happened, Peter found himself aboard *Black Joke*. Not knowing what else to do, he bent down and began shifting crates of salt cod. Somebody stepped on his feet, and someone else heaved a box that narrowly missed his head. There were too many men on deck for efficient work, and they were getting in each other's way. Frightened by the tumult and by the danger of discovery, Peter began to work his way through the press of shouting, heaving men until he reached the rail not far from a brand-new wheelhouse which had been erected near the stern of the ship. Suddenly a flashlight shone full in his face and his heart nearly stopped; but the light moved on at once and then Smith's voice bellowed almost in his ear.

"You, Jake, you blindin' idiot! You've got that cargo hoist rigged like a piece of knittin'. Don't you Brooklyn cowboys know *anything* about a sailin' ship? My God, if the engine ever quits, the lot of us'll drown . . . !"

There followed a string of profanity which made Peter's hair lift, and which sent him skittering over the rail and running headlong down the wharf. He was brought up short by collision with a pony — doing the pony no harm, but knocking the wind out of himself. He decided he had had enough for the moment and, still gasping for breath, headed for the churchyard. He was almost there when inspiration struck him.

"Kye . . . Jacques," he whispered as he slid in amongst the tombstones. "Where ye at? It's me, Peter."

"Over here," someone whispered back. It was Kye, crouched in the shadow of a headstone.

"I got aboard," Peter whispered excitedly. "Right onto her. They've changed her quite a bit. Got a wheelhouse onto her and new hatches. But listen, I know how to fix 'em good and maybe git the schooner back ourselves. . . . *Shhhh* — someone's sneakin' through the grass."

The "someone" was Jacques, and in a few moments he was squatting beside the other two while Peter poured out his plan.

"I heard Captain Smith talkin' with the crew, callin' 'em about forty red-hot names and sayin' they didn't know enough about a sailing ship to come across the harbor. He said if the engine ever quit, he figured they'd all drown. Well, I'm goin' to stow away until they start, and then I'm goin' to *make* that engine quit!"

"What good'll that do?" Kye asked skeptically.

"Do? Why it'll stop 'em cold! There ain't enough wind tonight to sail a dory, supposin' them robbers *did* know how to sail. If their engine quits after they git out in the bay they won't be able to come back, and they won't be able to go away neither. Now listen . . . Pierre's bound to git back here sometime soon. He's *bound* to, everybody says so. Jacques, ye tell him what I've done. Then he can come out with the dorymen and offer Smith a tow; and that'll be the end of Smith."

Jacques interrupted. "I do not like to say it," he said softly. "But I am very worried about my father. Maybe he does not come back. Maybe something bad has happened to him in St. Pierre. Then what will happen to you, eh?"

Peter shook his head with wild impatience.

"It don't *matter*," he almost shouted. "If their engine's bust, they still can't git far. Some other vessel's bound to pass close aboard. Maybe one of the New-foundland cutters even. And if I'm hid on board *Black Joke* and if I fires off a signal flare . . . That'll do it . . ." His voice faded off, for he could not really visualize what would follow such an action, even if it proved feasible.

"Ye're mad-crazy in the head," Kye said. "If we knowed Pierre was comin' for sure, it just might work. But if he don't come and ye stow away, that'll be the end of you. Maybe them fellers *can't* sail good, but I bet they can put canvas onto her somehow. And where ye goin' to git any signal flare? And what ye think they'll do to ye, when they finds ye . . . *and* they'll find ye certain sure. Ye and me's supposed to be dead, remem-ber? What's to stop 'em makin' ye *real* dead?"

"Kye is right," Jacques added. "It is too dangerous, it will not work. Where would you hide, eh? In so small a ship, there will be no place to hide. And how will you break the engine?"

Although Peter's common sense told him that the other two were right, he was so feverishly excited by the necessity of taking some action to regain possession of the ship that he refused to listen to reason. His face was set in hard lines that belonged to a much older person.

"All right, it's dangerous. But it *will* work. I can hide in the chain locker, and no one will ever know I'm there till I show myself. *And* I knows how to stop a diesel too. Ye only got to bust the fuel injectors with a hammer and the whole thing's finished.

"I'm *goin'* to do it, ye hear me? And don't try to stop

me neither. You just tell Pierre what I done, and he'll help me, even if you two won't."

Peter sprang suddenly to his feet and was away, running into darkness, before the other two could move.

"He's gone potty as a puffin," Kye cried. "C'mon, we got to stop him 'fore he gits hisself killed!"

Stopping Peter was not so easy. He had vanished amongst the confusion of men and ponies on the wharf, and though the two boys searched for fifteen minutes they found no trace of him. Finally they bumped into each other, and Kye muttered in Jacques' ear: "The blame fool must have done it. He must have gone aboard and into the locker. We can't haul him out of there without lettin' the whole world in on it — not if he won't come on his own, and I figure he won't."

"I think there is nothing we *can* do," Jacques replied.

Kye's eyes glittered in the momentary illumination of a match, as someone lit a cigarette.

"Well, there's one thing *I* can do," he said. "Go along with him. I got to do that much. I can't let him try it alone. Thank'ee Jacques. Ye've been a good feller; and I sure hope for all our sakes ye're dad gits back tonight."

Jacques clutched at Kye's jacket in an attempt to stop him, but Kye wrenched free with one quick movement.

He gained the deck without any difficulty. The salt fish had all been unloaded and a steady stream of whiskey boxes was being passed along from hand to hand by several men while others sweated below decks, stowing them away. There was less confusion on deck than when Peter had first come aboard, but there was still enough to mask Kye's movements as he slipped forward, cautiously slid off the small hatch which gave access to the chain locker and slid himself through it. His feet touched the pile of anchor chain and instantly he was grabbed about the knees and thrown heavily down while someone began scrambling over him towards the still-open hatch.

"Peter . . . Peter . . . lay off . . . it's Kye," he managed to gasp.

"Kye! I thought ye was one of the crew, and I figured I was a gonner. Kye, I'm scared to death!"

"Let's git out of here quick then. I'm so scared I figure me hair's turning green."

"No, Kye, I ain't goin'. I'm goin' to do what I said I'd do."

There was silence for a moment and then Kye sighed.

"Well," he said, "I guess that makes two of us. We're in for it together. Might as well git comfortable and have a think."

The space they were in was right in the bow of the ship, and the only openings into it were the small hatch and the two hawsepipes which led the chain down from the windlass. There was not enough room to stand up nor to stretch out. As Kye put it, "There ain't room to swing a mackerel." No light could enter, and precious little air. The stink of bilge and of old harbor mud from the chain cable was almost suffocating. Nevertheless, the two boys made themselves as comfortable as they could, sitting cross-legged on the pile of rusty chain with their backs against the thin bulkhead which separated the chain locker from the forepeak. Once or twice they heard someone clatter down the ladder into the forepeak, then go on deck again.

"We ain't goin' to be able to make no more noise than a butterfly in here," muttered Kye, "else anyone in the forepeak's bound to hear us."

"That's so," Peter replied, "but it works both ways. We'll be able to hear 'em talkin' in there, and that way we'll know their plans."

Kye snorted. "Plans! We knows right now what *their* plans are. Sail this lot of whiskey over to the States. What *we* got to do is make some plans. How ye figure we can git at the engine anyway?"

This was a detail which Peter had not yet considered.

"Don't know," he admitted reluctantly.

They sat in miserable silence for several minutes.

Peter was remembering what he had seen of the changes made to the boat by the rum-runners — changes he had noticed during his brief tour as a cargo handler on deck.

"Maybe after they git under way one of us can sneak aft," he suggested tentatively. "They'll be runnin' without lights till they gits well clear of Miquelon. And more'n likely most of the crew'll knock off to their bunks. We'll know about *that* because we'll hear 'em come down into the forepeak. The thing is, they've built a wheelhouse onto her, and it looked to me like the engine-room companion's been shifted to *abaft* the wheelhouse. So once ye got past the helmsman there'd be no one to see ye slip down into the engine room."

The two boys were talking in almost normal tones now, for there was so much noise on deck that no one could have heard them in any case. In fact they could hardly hear each other. But suddenly Kye caught Peter's arm in a hard grip.

"Watch out," he whispered sharply into his friend's ear. "The hatch!"

They both stared up. A slit of starlight showed where before there had been only darkness, for Peter had slid the hatch back into position immediately after he had recognized Kye.

The slit got wider, then the hatch-opening darkened as a head and shoulders blocked the entrance. Almost afraid to breathe, the two boys waited for the moment of discovery.

"Peter!" a voice whispered so softly they could hardly hear it. Trembling with relief, Peter and Kye scrambled to their feet and tried to push their faces out the hatch together.

They almost bumped heads with Jacques.

"Let me in. Quickly," he said. "But take this bag; we will need it, I think."

In a moment he had slid down beside them and Kye had replaced the hatch.

"One more scare like that and I'm just goin' to give up and die," Kye said shakily, when the three of them had got sorted out and had found room to sit in the cramped quarters. "What in the name of old Beelzebub are *you* doin' here, Jacques?"

"I think I do the same as you. You see, when you two

run away I don't know what I must do. Then I think I am your friend and also I know what my father will say if I let you go on the boat alone. So then I go to the fish store and light the candle and make a letter for my father. Only I have no paper so I write on a piece of wood. Then I take some things and put them in the bag. Then I go quick to the house and put the wood outside the door where my father or *ma mère* will see it when daylight comes. Then I come here."

"Well," Kye said, "I guess that makes *three* crazy nuts. What'd ye bring with ye, anyway?"

"I have one knife and some matches. I have also one bottle of wine and some ship biscuits *mon père* keep in the fish store for to take on the dory when he forget his lunch. Also a hammer for the engine. Also, Peter speaks of a signal flare, but there is none like that in the fish store so I bring instead a can of powder my father use to fill his shotgun shells."

"Gunpowder! You figure to blow up the ship?"

"But no, Kye. It will just burn very bright, and not make any bang unless it is in the cartridge case. It will be a good signal, you will see."

In the meanwhile things were progressing on deck. Only a few more cases of whiskey remained to be loaded — which was just as well, for Captain Benjamin Smith's temper was becoming explosive. He wished to be clear away from the French islands and far out to seaward before the dawn revealed his presence in these waters.

In his impatience he was not inclined to be polite. When a fisherman stumbled and dropped a case of whiskey so that it broke open, Smith was on him in two jumps and, picking him up by the scruff of his neck and the seat of his pants, he flung the unfortunate fellow headlong onto the wharf.

There were ugly murmurs from those who had witnessed the incident, and all work came slowly to a halt. Smith did not know it, or perhaps he simply did not care, but to lay violent hands on a Basque is as dangerous as prodding a rattlesnake.

Smith stepped to the rail and shone his flashlight over the fishermen.

"C'mon, c'mon!" he yelled at them. "Get that stuff on board!"

Not a man moved, and something of the menace in their silence began to seep through even Smith's tough skin.

"Okay," he said loudly. "No work, no pay. Jake, have our boys sling the rest of those cases on the ship."

Two or three of the rum-runners stepped onto the wharf to obey the order, but the fishermen moved solidly forward and the surprised sailors suddenly found themselves back on board again.

"You will pay what you owe, *capitain*," said a voice from the crowd.

"The blazes I will!" Smith replied. "Leave them last few cases lay, Jake. Cast off them lines. Greasy, get that engine going. Gabby! Gabby! Where in the name of darkness is that Frog pilot?"

"I am on shore, *capitain*," Gabby Morazi replied,

"and I *stay* ashore. I am only a Frog, you see, and therefore I cannot possibly pilot your ship."

"I can't cast off them lines, Ben," Jake interjected into the silence that followed Gabby's announcement. "The Frogs won't let me get ashore."

"Cut the blank things then, cut 'em *now!* We're movin' out, you hear?"

The diesel suddenly burst into life; and before the fishermen could make a move, the three mooring lines had been sliced through and *Black Joke* was moving away from the dock.

Down in the chain locker the boys heard the shouts being exchanged between the deck and the wharf. Although they had not been able to catch all that was said, they had heard enough to realize that Captain Smith was no longer in favor with the local people. This knowledge helped to brace their spirits, which had begun to plummet as the diesel started and as they felt the ship begin to move. They were committed now — there was no going back.

13

The Battle for *Black Joke*

IT WAS shortly before 2:00 A.M. when *Black Joke* pulled clear of the little wharf. Captain Smith was in a foul mood. Having lost his pilot, he realized that he would now be forced to sound every inch of the way out of Miquelon Bay in order to avoid the shoals; and in order to sound he would have to steam dead slow.

Standing in the wheelhouse he stuck his head out the port window and slung a string of curses at his mate, the man called Jake.

"You name of a New Jersey name!" he bellowed. "Get two of those blanking clodhoppers forward with lead lines. I want the depth called every swing, and I want a swing every fifteen seconds. Now *jump* or by the blankety four blanks I'll move you with some *hot* lead!"

Jake jumped, and in a moment the three boys in the chain locker heard the pounding of feet overhead, and soon afterwards the monotonous calling of the depth began as two sailors swung their lead lines alternately.

"Three fathoms . . . three and a half . . . four."

"That tears it," Kye whispered. "Goin' out on his own by the lead. Them two fellers is right above our heads and we ain't got a chance to sneak out on deck and git aft to the engine room without they see us. How long ye reckon he'll have to use the lead, Jacques, considerin' he don't know the way?"

"There are shoals right to the mouth of the bay, Kye. In the dark he will be wise to take soundings until he is past Miquelon Head."

"That means we'll be clear out to sea fore we can even try to git out of here," Peter whispered miserably. "Ye was right, you two. I'm ten kinds of a fool. We never should have come aboard. I'm right sorry I got ye into this, I'm sorry. . . ."

"Pickle it, Peter," Kye interrupted abruptly. "We're here, and them fellers don't *know* we're here so we're not beat yet. Now git thinkin' — git thinkin' hard. There's got to be somethin' we can do."

But there was nothing they could do. They were trapped for as long as the two leadsmen stood on the deck above them, and it looked as if the men would be there until daylight, by which time it would be impossible to try to reach the engine room.

However, the boys had a hidden ally they did not know about, a totally unexpected one — none other than Captain Smith himself.

Two hours after *Black Joke* had left the dock, Smith's slim store of patience ran out. For two hours he had kept the vessel creeping through the darkness like a tired snail. He could stand no more of it. He was reasonably sure he was clear of the worst shoals, and as for the rest — well, the ship would have to take her chances.

He shoved the speed control handle to full throttle and again stuck his head out the wheelhouse window and shouted to his mate who was with the two leadsmen. "Okay, Jake. Call off them houn' dogs you got bayin' in the bow. Tell your loafin' bunch of bums they can all turn in — them as ain't asleep on their feet already. I'll take her myself till dawn. You rustle me up some coffee."

This time the three boys heard almost every word of what was shouted. They listened intently to the thump of boots as men came heavily down the ladder into the forepeak. They sat quite still while the crew rumbled about behind the bulkhead. They heard a brief and uncomplimentary discussion of Captain Smith's nature, his ancestors, and his probable future; and the sound of corks being drawn from bottles. Then, one by one, the rum-runners crawled into their berths. In a few more minutes the sound of snoring had grown almost as loud as the sound of the diesel. Only one man was still awake: the mate, who was brewing a pot of coffee.

Kye drew the other two boys' heads down close to his.

"This is it," he muttered. "Never be a better chance. Who's goin' to have a shot at it?"

"I'm the one, and that's flat," Peter said and, though his voice was taut with fear, there was no question but that he meant it.

"Wait, please," Jacques whispered. "I have been thinking. How will you get past the wheelhouse, Peter? The *capitain,* he will surely see you, *non?* And the man, Jake, he may return on deck also. So, we must make them not to see you. Put your hands down here . . . there is a hole in the bulkhead, do you feel it? . . . A rat-hole perhaps. If we pour some powder through that hole and put a match to it . . . *poooff!* . . . there will be a big flash. The forepeak will be full of smoke. The men will think the ship is on fire. They will yell and jump out. I think the *capitain* will run forward too. If you, Peter, are hiding close to the wheelhouse at that time you will have a chance to pass by to the engine room without trouble, I think. It is good, eh? *Bien,* after you go on deck, Kye and I will wait as long as it takes to count one hundred. If we hear nothing, we will know you are all right. Then we will light the powder."

"By the Harry, ye sure got a head for thinkin'," Kye whispered admiringly. "What about it, Peter?"

"Start gittin' your powder ready, Jacques, and hand me the hammer, Kye. You fellers keep the knife in case . . . in case. I got to go right now. If I waits another minute I'll be so scared I'll be stiff as a dead cod. You ready yet, Jacques?"

In the darkness Jacques could not tell how much powder he was pouring through the hole. He had to be certain it was enough to cause a real diversion. In order to be sure, he tilted the can sharply one final time.

"You'll make it, Peter. I *knows* ye will," Kye whispered as Peter gently slid back the hatch, thrust his head out for a quick look, then wriggled up and out of sight.

It was a magnificent night. Only a little zephyr of a breeze rippled the black waters about the vessel as she drove steadily out to sea. Thin clouds obscured some of the stars, but enough of them remained so that Peter, now thoroughly accustomed to darkness, could see quite well. There was a dim light in the wheelhouse, probably a reflection from the binnacle lamp, and by it he could see Captain Smith's head behind the glass.

Taking a long, deep breath, Peter bent double and cautiously moved aft, counting to himself as he went. He passed the open slider of the forepeak companion and smelled the coffee boiling. Just in time, he thought with a shiver. In another minute or two the mate would be coming on deck again. Twenty, twenty-one, twenty-two — he reached the starboard side of the main hatch and, getting down on his hands and knees, began to crawl along in the shelter of it. Forty-seven, forty-eight — he was halfway to the mainmast now, and less than twenty feet from the wheelhouse; but where was he going to hide? He could not guess which side of the ship Smith would come along when the powder went off — sixty-three, sixty-four — something loomed in front of him, and his hands went out to it quickly. It was a loosely coiled mooring line. Almost without thinking, Peter wriggled into the middle of the coil and pulled some of the loops over him — ninety-five . . . ninety-nine . . . one hundred-and-three — his hands were icy with sweat, and the hammer, which he had shoved into his belt and which was now beneath him, was hurting his leg intolerably — one hundred-and-ten — *what* had gone wrong? He couldn't stand this for much longer; he was so close to the wheelhouse that if Smith looked his way he couldn't help but see him. One hundred-and-fift —

A great flash of white light seemed to leap out of the open forepeak companionway, and for a moment the whole ship stood out in brilliant detail. There was a muffled *whoomf* from forward that shook the vessel as if she had run into something solid, and then the night was filled with shrieks and yells.

Peter saw the wheelhouse door flung open and Smith come lumbering toward him. Smith had been looking forward when the powder went off and had received the full effect of the sudden glare. Almost blinded, he rushed forward, yelling unanswerable questions over the cacophony of human voices which was pouring out of the companionway through a swirling cloud of smoke. Abruptly his foot caught in the coil of rope and he pitched full length across Peter, striking his forehead against the edge of the main hatch. It was a severe blow, but it did not knock him out.

Cursing, Smith managed to get to his knees, dragging his legs right across Peter, and then he began crawling forward on his hands and knees, having completely failed to notice the boy.

Peter was shaking so badly that his body would not

obey him. He knew there was very little time before the occupants of the forepeak would all come scrambling out on deck. He took his lip between his teeth and deliberately bit it as hard as he could. Pain shot through him like an electric shock, and his uncontrolled shivering ceased. Then he was on his feet, running the last dozen paces.

The engine-room scuttle was closed but not locked, and he flung it open and plunged down the short stairs. The thunder of the diesel filled his ears — *but he could not see*. He had forgotten that there might be no light in the engine room. Frantically he thrust his hands into the worn pockets of the fisherman's trousers he had borrowed. His fingers touched and grasped a match, one match. He knew it might have been there for months, might have been wet a score of times, and might now be quite useless. His trembling was returning as he knelt and felt for a dry place on the floor. He scratched the match . . . too carefully . . . try again . . . there was a faint hiss, a blue glow, and then, miraculously, he could see. His eyes searched the engine-room walls for a light switch, and just as the match began to burn his fingers and die down, he saw it. Lunging for it he pulled the toggle and the light went on.

Now he could hear the yells of men even above the thunder of the engine which stood before him. The deck vibrated with footsteps. Someone was coming aft at a dead run. Well, they were too late.

He stepped forward and very deliberately swung his

hammer at the first injector. Fuel oil spurted in all directions. Six cylinders, six injectors — one . . . two . . . three . . . four . . . five . . . six. The ragged thunder of the diesel died to silence.

Down in the chain locker Jacques had counted slowly in order to give Peter lots of time. When he reached one hundred, he took out a match scratched it on the chain at his feet, and as coolly as a man lighting a cigarette, bent over and touched the powder train.

Now, there are many kinds of gunpowder. The common kind is black, burns slowly, and is fairly harmless unless it is ignited in a closed container. Another kind is white and sugarlike in appearance and is used for high velocity cartridge loads. It is *never* harmless, and it burns so fast that even in the open the effect can be explosive. The powder in Jacques's can had been white — but in the darkness, how was he to tell?

The resultant *whoomf* as the powder ignited was so powerful that even in the chain locker it almost knocked the two boys down. It blew the hatch above their heads clean off and sent it sailing overboard. A cloud of bitter, choking smoke billowed back at them through cracks in the bulkhead and sent them coughing wildly and in panic-stricken flight out of the now open hatch. They reached the deck and, crouching just forward of the windlass, listened horrified to the sounds from the forepeak.

Had Jacques been a little more generous with the

powder, the explosion would probably have been fatal to some of the men in the forepeak. As things stood, they were reasonably well protected because the blast took place beneath their bunks. Nevertheless, the concussion was enough to half-stun them, and the acrid, rolling smoke nearly asphixiated them before they could recover their senses. Yelling and screaming in pure terror, they stumbled into and over one another as they fought desperately to find the ladder and escape from the shambles of the forepeak. Someone hit his head against the gimballed oil lamp, which had been blown out by the blast. He struck it such a blow that he split his own scalp and sent the lamp tumbling down upon the stovetop. A trickle of kerosene began to flow from the lamp's brass reservoir into the crack of a stovelid, and a tongue of yellow flame instantly licked up into the smoke-filled darkness.

The last man up the ladder saw that flame and as he crawled out into the pandemonium of cursing and coughing men he raised a fear-filled voice in the most dreaded cry that can be heard at sea.

"She's afire below! She's goin' t' go! For God's sake, get the boat over. . . . *She's goin' to go!*"

Black Joke's crew were demoralized anyway — being blown out of one's bed in the small hours of the morning is enough to shake the courage of any man — but the cry of fire put the cap on it. Every man aboard knew what would happen if the cargo burned. Twelve thousand exploding bottles of overproof spirits would turn the ship into a flaming torch within a matter of minutes. Brute panic overwhelmed the crew at this prospect, and they stampeded aft.

The blast had not only forced the powder smoke into the chain locker, but into the main hold abaft the fore-peak as well. It was now seeping out through the badly secured main hatch. The mate, who was the only rela-tively rational man of the lot — and the only one with enough presence of mind to grab a flashlight before crawling on deck — might even then have managed to regain some control of the crew, but as the men began to run past him he swung the beam of his flashlight and caught a glimpse of the wisps of smoke curling up from the edge of the cargo hatch. At the same moment he be-came aware that the engine had stopped.

Panic is infectious. Instead of trying to stem the rush to reach the boat, Jake joined it. There was no time or inclination to reason things out. For all he knew the entire ship below decks, including the engine room, was probably afire. He had no intention of remaining aboard to find out, or of trying to stem the fire single-handedly. As for Smith, his Captain — well, Smith could look out for himself if he hadn't already done so.

Panic was now unrestrained, and the belief that the ship might soon blow up crowded out every other thought save the terrible need to get as far away from *Black Joke* as possible in the shortest conceivable time.

The crew did not launch the boat, which was slung on davits in the stern; they simply threw it overboard and jumped after it. As they heaved themselves out of the water and into the boat, they were so completely demoralized that they half-swamped it and lost several of the oars. Screaming and cursing at each other, they tried frantically to get the boat under way.

Meantime, Smith had regained his feet and was staggering aft. He was dazed, and suffering considerable pain. Blood was running freely down the side of his face. He had not yet been able to form any clear idea of what had happened, or was happening to the vessel. But one thing he understood — his crew was abandoning ship without his order.

Despite his moral lapses Smith *was* a good seaman, a master mariner, and no coward. Neither explosion nor fire could drive him to abandon his vessel while a chance of saving her remained. He intended to fight for *Black Joke,* but in order to do so he needed the assistance of his crew.

Black Joke still had some way on her and was slowly pulling away from the lifeboat, which was now almost lost to sight in the darkness. Smith knew there was no point in simply ordering the men back or even in trying to persuade them to return. He had seen enough of panic in his day not to underestimate its power. There was only one thing he could try and he did not hesitate. Pulling out his automatic, he fired two shots close over the heads of the seething mob in the boat.

"Back to the ship," he bellowed, "or I'll drill the rotten lot of you!"

It was a desperate threat. The boat was barely visible and almost out of pistol range. Someone had got a pair of oars between the tholepins and was already rowing hard. Yet the threat might just possibly have worked if a tongue of flame had not chosen that moment to come licking up out of the forepeak companionway, momentarily illuminating most of the forward part of the ship and clearly revealing the curling plumes of powder smoke still rising from the chain locker and the main hatch.

It also illuminated, briefly, the strained faces of the men in the boat. Then it died down, and there was a demented babble of cries as more oars struck the water and the men pulled with frantic desperation away from the apparently doomed ship.

Smith wasted no more time upon his crew, for they

were gone. Cursing fluently, he staggered to the engine room companion, flung wide the door, and started down the stairs to get the big foam extinguisher which hung beside the engine.

The whole course of events since the explosion had occupied only four or five minutes, but to Peter, crouching beside the silent diesel, it had seemed like many hours. Having done what he had set out to do, he now had no idea what to do next. He could not think, but could only listen appalled to the pandemonium on deck, to the shrieks and yells, and finally to the pistol shots and the great bellow from Captain Smith. Realization that the ship actually was afire penetrated into his frightened mind only very slowly, but at the moment when Smith flung back the companion doors and started down the ladder, Peter had begun to understand the danger. The lifeboat was gone, the ship was on fire; he *had* to get on deck. He ran straight into Smith's arms.

Smith must have been immensely surprised, but he had no time to indulge it.

"You! Whoever you are!" he said fiercely. "Get forward. There's fire buckets abaft the foremast. Start heavin' water down the forepeak as if your life was on it. GIT!" He half-flung Peter up the stairs, and the boy was already running by the time he reached the deck. There was light to see by now, a flickering red glow from the forepeak companion. So much had happened to Peter by this time that he was almost numb.

One thought remained in his head . . . fire buckets abaft the foremast.

He reached the buckets, and out of the darkness forward two figures rose up as one and ran to meet him. In the glow of the fire he could see two terrified sets of eyes gleaming at him.

"Buckets!" he yelled, and grabbing one himself he caught the lanyard in one hand and heaved the red pail overboard. Jacques and Kye needed no second telling. Within seconds they too were throwing buckets overboard, hauling them up full, and dashing the contents down the open companionway.

The sharp crackle and the glare of flame told them that the fire was well into the woodwork. Coiling clouds of smoke mingling with gusts of scorching air were now billowing freely out of the companionway so that they had to heave the water into it from a distance of several feet. Seen by the reflected glow of the flames, they seemed like three maniac dwarfs as they scuttled back and forth between the rail and the companionway.

What Captain Smith must have thought, as he lumbered onto the scene with a big foam extinguisher under his arm, remained unexpressed. He had no time to consider how one unexplained boy hiding in the engine room had suddenly become three.

"I'm goin' down," he bawled at them. "Keep them buckets comin' and heave 'em over me. Wet me down good and keep doin' it or we'll all of us finish up with the devil tonight!"

Unslinging the extinguisher he grasped the nozzle

and turned toward the companionway. A full pail of water flung by Kye caught him on the head and ran down his neck. A second pailful drenched his shoulders. He waited until three more pailfuls had been flung over him and then, hauling the top of his turtle-necked jersey up over his face and pulling his peaked cap down over his eyes, he hunched his shoulders and stepped deliberately into the smoke-filled opening.

"He'll burn to death!" Kye screamed.

"The water! Keep it comin'!" Peter yelled hysterically. "Keep him wet down!"

Now the three boys moved with the fury of madmen. Pail after pail of salt water whooshed through the opening. They moved in so close to the companionway that the smoke half-blinded them while the heat seared their faces. Panting and sweating like exhausted dogs, they were only half aware of what they were doing now. They hardly noticed the subdued hissing sound of the extinguisher which was beginning to be heard over the failing crackle of the fire; and they were only vaguely aware that it was getting darker — that the red glare was dying down. Smoke billowed much more thickly from the opening, but now it was only smoke, and no more flame.

They continued heaving water like mindless robots. Rushing back from the rail, Peter was about to swing his bucket toward the companionway when he realized that there was something moving in the opening. It looked like an arm waving slowly and then falling, to lie limply on the deck. There was almost no light now, and he was not quite sure what he had seen, but he dropped the bucket, reached forward groping, touched a hand, and yelled. "He's tryin' to git out! Help me, b'ys!"

Jacques was by his side in an instant. Together they began hauling at the limp arm. Kye joined them and the three boys strained at the inert bulk of the man and slowly dragged him up, over the sill, and out into the open.

Smith's cap was gone and his hair was singed down to his scalp, but he had not suffered serious burns, except to his hands. The steady flow of water from above had saved him from the heat, but the combination of smoke and carbon dioxide from the extinguisher had been too much for even his massive strength. Beginning to pass out, he had just been able to climb the ladder to the companion entrance before he became unconscious.

Jacques bent over him and listened to the ragged, heavy breathing.

"I think he is all right. But the fire maybe is not yet out! We must keep on!"

Though almost totally exhausted, the boys returned automatically to their task. They had lost all track of time. Mechanically they staggered to the rail, dipped their buckets, and staggered back. They had no breath to spare for even a single word to one another. Had they paused and looked, they would have seen that the fire was out, for the carbon dioxide had smothered the flames effectively and the steady flood of water had killed the last glowing embers. But they did not stop until Peter, with a groan, slipped down in a dead faint.

The clatter of his bucket rolling across the deck was like a signal freeing Jacques and Kye from a nightmare. They too dropped their buckets and sank to the deck in a state of near collapse.

14

The Long Voyage Ends

It was past three o'clock in the morning before Pierre Roulett breasted the last rise and began making his way painfully down the mountain slopes toward the village. He was very tired but the sight of a number of lights moving through the village streets made him hurry his pace.

"Hello!" he cried as he approached a man carrying a storm lantern. "What you looking for at this time of night, eh?"

"Is that you, Pierre? *Bon!* There is much trouble. Jacques and the boys of *Terre Neuve* have disappeared. The whole of Miquelon is out looking for them. Pascal waits at your house. He will tell you what has happened."

Pascal was standing just inside the kitchen door when Pierre burst in. The young man was trying to defend himself from a verbal assault by Mrs. Roulett, who seemed almost on the point of going for him with her bare hands.

"Stop that screeching!" Pierre bellowed in a voice that brooked no opposition. "What has happened here, Pascal?"

Much relieved by Pierre's arrival, but still eying the infuriated Mrs. Roulett apprehensively, Pascal broke into a rapid explanation of all that had occurred up to the moment when *Black Joke* had been cut loose from the dock and had vanished into darkness. At this point he was interrupted by Marie, who could no longer contain herself.

"I warned they lads not to go nigh the wharf whilst the schooner was layin' there," she cried in English. "But that fool, Pascal, he let 'em go. If they've come to any hurt, I'll reach his scalp right off his head!"

"Be quiet, woman!" Pierre shouted. "What do you *think* has happened to them, Pascal?"

"They are not in the village, or near it, Pierre. It seems impossible, but the only place they *can* be is aboard the ship."

"When did she sail?" Pierre snapped.

"An hour and a half ago, but without a pilot. We told Gabby Morazi the plan was off when you did not appear, and so he decided to stay ashore. The schooner must be steaming dead slow, feeling her way with the leadline through the shoals. Already we have been thinking of going after her. . . ."

"*Thinking!*" Pierre interrupted harshly. "Why did you not *act?* Find me twelve men and the three fastest dories on the beach. And whatever guns you can grab quick. I give you five minutes only. *Go!*"

Pierre himself remained behind only long enough to snatch up his shotgun and a handful of shells, then he was off for the beach. He had already winched his own dory into the water before the other men appeared.

"Make the course toward Miquelon Head," he ordered curtly. "Smith will steer that way for sure. Pascal, you try and keep a quarter-mile to port of me. Uncle Paul, you keep a quarter-mile to starboard."

Moments later the dories were under way. At the helm of his own boat Pierre sat tense and grim. He knew the odds were heavily against catching up with the schooner, unless by some freak she happened to put herself on a shoal. He also knew, having heard about the row at the wharf, that Smith would be wary about letting any dory come close to him.

The boats drove noisily through the darkness, and every eye was strained for some indication that would lead the pursuit toward the fleeing schooner. Yet the men were totally unprepared when, with fearful abruptness, a flare of white light burst up from the surface of the sea far ahead of them and hung flickering for an instant like a flash of summer lightning.

Pierre was the first to realize what it was they had seen. "*Sacré bleu!*" he cried in anguish, "It is the ship! She has blown up!"

As if by a common impulse, the three dories drew in upon each other until they were running almost gunwale to gunwale toward the site of the distant flash where now a flickering red glow had come into being.

"Pray God they can get off in time!" One of the men

aboard Pierre's dory yelled above the sound of the laboring engine. "She will be a torch in a few minutes. . . . Pray God . . . !"

There was nothing else to do but pray. In each dory, men crouched down, leaning forward as if they could will the boats to a faster speed. Pierre's hand on the tiller was clenched so tightly that some of his fingernails broke off, but he did not even notice. . . .

Aboard the schooner Kye painfully opened his eyes and sat up. It seemed to him that he had been asleep for hours, dreaming wildly of an explosion and leaping flames, though in reality he had slept only a few minutes. The sound of heavy groans had wakened him, and now he saw that Smith was sitting near, holding both burned hands in front of him so that they bore a ghastly resemblance to two freshly boiled lobsters. The sight of those hands brought Kye fully to his senses. His fear and hatred of Smith were submerged in a wave of horrified pity.

"Hang on, sorr," he cried. "I'll run aft and git some grease out of the engine room. It'll maybe help some to ease the pain."

Smith looked over at the boy and, despite his agony, he grinned.

"Grease is it, you young scut? More likely you'll stick a knife in me ribs and finish me off. When it comes to fightin' a bunch of young devils what don't even mind blowin' themselves to glory to hijack a ship, I quit! This boat's all yours, sonny. . . . Only lay off the dynamite, will you?"

Despite himself, Kye could not help returning the grin, though a bit shamefacedly.

"I guess we're sorry," he said slowly. "We never meant to hurt nobody. It was just that we *had* to stop ye gittin' clear."

"Okay," Smith replied. "You stopped me. Now fetch that grease. Then you better wake up your pals there, and take charge of this hulk before she ends up on the rocks and drowns us all. There's nothin' I can do to help nor hinder you."

But Smith *was* able to help. After Kye had smothered his burns in grease and had then shaken the other two boys awake, it was Smith who gave the orders.

"Cut loose that starboard anchor," he told them, "and let run about fifteen fathoms of chain. Then one of you light the gas lantern that's in the wheelhouse. Hang it in the rigging as high as you can climb. There's flares too. Fire one of 'em every ten minutes. The Frogs ashore will see 'em and come out for loot, if nothing else."

Groggily, and still half-stupefied with exhaustion, the boys did as Smith directed. Jacques had just fired the third flare when the distant mutter of dory engines made itself heard. The boys shouted hopefully into the darkness and fired the remaining flares with the abandon of a fireworks display.

Fifteen minutes later the dories loomed alongside. Seconds afterwards Pierre leapt aboard, shotgun in his

hand and his big electric torch sweeping the decks which were already growing dimly visible in the pre-dawn light.

The boys clustered around him, almost hysterical with relief. But Pierre only lingered with them long enough to assure himself they were all right before striding over to the main hatch where Smith was sitting. Pierre lifted the shotgun and swung it until the muzzle was only inches away from the American's head.

"I theenk you bettair say your prayers pretty quick, *monsieur le kidnappair!*" he said tautly.

Smith did not flinch from the threat.

"Kidnaper, nothin'!" he replied with feeling. "It was them *kids* done the napin'. Drove off my crew, hijacked my boat, and damn near got me burned to a crisp into the bargain! Mister, there ain't nothin' you can do to me that they ain't already thought of!"

Meanwhile Jacques had jumped to his father's side and pulled down the muzzle of the gun. In rapid French he described what had happened from the moment Peter decided to stow away aboard *Black Joke*. Pierre and the other fisherman listened in incredulous silence to the tale. By the time Jacques finished, the hard lines on Pierre's face had softened.

"By Gar, *capitain*," he said. "You have easier time if you ship the cargo of wolf cubs, eh? I thank you for save these fool boys' lives when you put out the fire, but you mus' realize the boat she don' belong to you no more. You fellows steal her from my fren' *capitain* Spence — now the boys take her back, is it not so?"

"I won't give you no argument. That guy Spence can

have his boat back for all of me. Just ask him not to sic them kids onto me again!"

"Bon," said Pierre, "but now I have business with the ship. One of the men here, he take you to Miquelon in hees dory. My wife Marie, she pretty good nurse an' she feex up those burns you got. . . . Hey, you boys! You go 'long with the dory too, 'fore you make more troubles on thees schooner."

Jacques was about to obey his father's order, but Peter turned stubborn.

"I'm sorry, Mister Roulette," he said. "I guess me and Kye better stay aboard. She's a Spence vessel and there ought to be a Spence onto her as long as she's at sea."

Pierre gave him a quizzical look.

"I hope you don' theenk the Basques try to steal her now," he said. "Okay, I suppose I get the devil from Marie for let you stay, but me, I don' feel strong enough to put you fellows off. Maybe you blow *me* up if I try that, eh?"

By this time daylight was strengthening and Pierre was anxious to be off, for the task of unloading and of hiding the schooner's cargo still remained. Calling Uncle Paul, he instructed the old man to take Smith ashore and then to gather a few men and round up the rest of the smugglers. Their lifeboat was now visible on the shore of the bay where the crew had landed after their panic-stricken flight from the burning ship.

As soon as Uncle Paul and Smith had left, Pierre or-

dered the two remaining dories to be made fast, one
on each side of *Black Joke*. The anchor was recovered
and then, propelled by the engines of the dories, *Black
Joke* slowly got under way toward the sea-caves on
the rugged eastern shore of Miquelon. It was a perfect
morning for the voyage. The water was calm and there
was a haze which cut visibility to a mile or so, and
effectively shielded the schooner from the sight of any
passing ships at sea.

At Pierre's orders, the boys made their way down
into the after cabin where they curled up on mattresses
and Smith's blankets and sank into a sleep of exhaustion. Nor did they wake until several hours later when
the sound of the dory engines was replaced by the
rattle of blocks and tackle and the noise of hatch covers
being removed. When they crawled sleepily on deck,
they found the schooner moored to the foot of a high
cliff with her bowsprit almost touching the rocks. A
few yards away to starboard the black mouth of a sea-
cave yawned and already one of the dories, piled high
with cases of whiskey, was being sculled toward it.

The boys volunteered to help unload the whiskey,
but were refused by Pierre. "Een one night you do
more than ten men do in a month," he told them.
"Now you take leetle holiday. Maybe you find your-
selve some food eef it don' all burn up in the fire."

Peter and Jacques climbed down into the gutted forepeak, and amongst the charred bedding and burned
gear they found some tins whose labels had vanished,
but which were still intact. When they brought these

on deck and opened them with a clasp knife they found they were filled with beans — doubly baked beans, and still warm from the fire.

Having satisfied some of their hunger pains, they cadged a ride aboard one of the dories and spent some time examining the cave where the whiskey was being stored. It was a dark, echoing slit in the mountains, extending back far beyond the reaches the boys cared to explore, even helped by Pierre's electric torch.

"My father says this place was used for contraband many years ago," Jacques told the others. "Before that, it was a place the pirates came to hide their treasure. Maybe the man who owned the first *Black Joke* — the one you tell me about — maybe he come here too."

"I bet Captain John Phillip wouldn't have thought too much of *this* kind of treasure," said Peter contemptuously, as he swung the beam of the torch over the stacks of whiskey cases which stood on a series of ledges well above the high-water mark.

"Maybe not," Kye replied. "I guess it ain't much like gold nor silver, but it'll still git *Black Joke* back all legal-like, *and* set yer father free and clear."

The work of unloading the whiskey continued through most of the morning, and the sun was beginning to burn away the haze before the last cases were ferried into the caves. Meanwhile Pierre and Pascal had been occupied in the engine room of *Black Joke*. They had found a spare set of injectors, thoughtfully provided by the provident Monsieur Gauthier in case of engine trouble at sea. These were quickly installed and though they had considerable trouble re-connecting the fuel lines, which had been well battered by Peter's hammer blows, they managed to complete the repairs in time to take the schooner away from the caves under her own power.

She steamed back into Miquelon Roads that afternoon, with Peter standing proudly at her wheel, while the other two boys clung to her mainmast rigging waving frenziedly at the people on the wharf. Almost the whole population of the village was on hand to greet the returning ship. Even Smith, his hands heavily bandaged, appeared on the dock. Word of how he had put out the fire had spread rapidly, and he was no longer looked upon with hostility by the fishermen, for they could appreciate a brave deed as well as anyone.

But Smith's crew was not in evidence. As Uncle Paul explained later, they had been trying to make their way over the mountains toward Langlade when they were terrified to discover a party of Basques, all armed with shotguns, pressing close on their heels.

"Silly fools!" Uncle Paul said, snorting with disdain. "Naturally we only took our guns along in case we met some game. But when those fellows saw us they ran like rabbits. In rubber sea-boots too! By the time we got them stopped, their feet were like raw turnips. We left them in a hunting cabin with two of our men to keep them from getting into mischief."

The reception accorded the boys and Pierre by Marie Roulett was not so triumphant as the one they had received at the wharf. She gave Pierre such a tongue-lashing that he withdrew in confusion to the peace of the beach. The boys, having been soundly scolded, were fed an enormous meal and then rushed off to bed. Marie suspiciously took their clothes away and hid them, so as to ensure that they stayed in bed.

"Ye'll sleep till I lets ye wake, ye sculpins!" she told them sternly. "And when ye wakes, I'll more 'an likely tan the three of ye for good measure."

The threat did not disturb the boys, but their dignity was a little hurt by the removal of their clothing. Considering that they were three pirates who had successfully hijacked a ship and her entire cargo, they felt that they were entitled to more respect from womankind — even from mothers. But they were too tired to be much perturbed and they were asleep almost as soon as they climbed into bed.

Pierre spent some time that evening talking to Smith, who agreed to carry the message to Gauthier, demanding Jonathan's release and the transfer of ownership of *Black Joke* back to him, in exchange for the return of the cargo of whiskey.

Smith was an energetic man who did not allow his injuries to hamper him. That very evening he left for St. Pierre in Pierre's boat, accompanied by Pascal. And in the middle of the following morning he was back in Miquelon. With him in the dory was Jonathan Spence, released from jail after his fine had been paid by Gauthier, and carrying in his pocket a brand-new bill of sale restoring legal ownership of *Black Joke* to him.

Pierre met them at the dock and, while Jonathan

went on ahead to the house, Pierre lingered for a few words with Smith.

"By Gar, that was fast work, my fren'!"

"No trouble," Smith replied modestly. "I just passed on the deal you offered. Maybe I helped a little, when I told 'em I was going to have a tough time persuading the big bosses in New Jersey that Gauthier didn't mastermind the whole hijack stunt himself. I wasn't lyin' none either. I don't guess the Big Boys is goin' to do much more business with Gauthier, but I reckon we can do business with you fellows once we get this mess patched up."

Pierre had to run to catch up to Jonathan, who was just entering the Roulett house, where he was warmly greeted by Marie. A few moments later her shrill voice brought Kye and Peter stumbling down the stairs, so excited that they forgot they were dressed only in their underwear. Jonathan caught them about the shoulders and hugged them to him with rough affection.

"Well, b'ys," he said, "I suppose I'll have to come back aboard *Black Joke* afore the mast . . . now that you two has took over as skipper and mate. Go find ye're trousers and then set down and let's hear the whole yarn."

So the story was told all over again, from its beginning on Colombier Rock; first in English, and with many mutual interruptions between Kye and Peter; then by Jacques in French for the benefit of an ever-increasing audience, for it seemed that most of the population of Miquelon had crowded into the Rouletts' big kitchen.

It was clear that the villagers intended to celebrate the recapture of *Black Joke* in true Basque fashion. Although Jonathan was anxious to return home as soon as possible, he found it hard to resist Pierre's pleadings to the effect that he and the boys should remain for at least another day.

"We don' wish you to go so soon, my fren'," Pierre cried. "Tonight all the people make the party and the dance for you — the special Basque dance. So you see you must stay; an' you won' lose no time either, because the boat she is feex up so good now she get you home before you know it. That new engine make her go like a whale. Gauthier, he don' spare the money when he has her on the slip. Everything aboard is new and of the best kind. I think he spend four thousand' dollar' for to feex her up. So now you got the finest boat on all the coast. That fire don' make no big damage — nothing you can't feex yourself in two, three days."

Before leaving St. Pierre for Miquelon Jonathan had dispatched a cable to Ship Hole in order to set his wife's mind at ease, so that he really had no good reason to refuse Pierre's enthusiastic invitation. Consequently all that day, and far into the night, he and the two boys were feasted and fêted, and even persuaded to take part in the hectic national dance of the Basques.

None of the three got up very early the next morning, but nevertheless *Black Joke* was ready to sail by noon, for the Basques had seen to all the preparations.

As Jonathan was preparing to go aboard, Pierre had a last word with him.

"This morning we stow the schooner with the salt fish Gauthier had aboard to hide *le whiskey,* so you see you don' go home empty-handed. And maybe you fin' a little special cargo buried under the fish. You have many fren's in Miquelon and they know about the hard times in *Terre Neuve.*"

Grasping Pierre's hand, Jonathan squeezed it so hard that the big Basque grunted with pain.

"Thank'ee, b'y," Jonathan said gruffly. "Words don't come aisy to I, but there's nothin' me nor mine won't do for you and yours if ever the time comes ye needs a hand."

"By Gar!" Pierre replied ruefully. "I think I need a hand right now! This one of mine, she is squash' like dead squid on the shore."

The departure was a boisterous affair. A gay crowd consisting of most of the people of Miquelon had gathered to see the schooner off. As the lines were let go, a score of shotguns roared out a farewell salute and a hundred voices were raised in a lusty Basque song. Peter and Kye replied by sounding repeated blasts on the ship's foghorn. Standing on the dock, as the schooner pulled slowly away, Jacques cupped his hands and yelled a final good-by to the two Newfoundland lads with whom he had become such close friends.

The wind was fresh from the southeast. Under the combined power of her sails and her diesel engine,

Black Joke was soon logging a full twelve knots. It was still daylight when she began to close with the shores of Newfoundland. The massive sea-cliffs rose up close ahead, and the roar of bursting seas echoed back from the great rocks. Snoring through the water, the black-hulled ship bore down through the shadows of the evening.

Black Joke was going home at last.